J FIC END
Enderle, Dotti, 1954-
Crosswire /
1st ed.

NE

FEB 2 9 2012

D1016945

CROSSWIRE

Dotti Enderle

CALKINS CREEK

HONESDALE • PENNSYLVANIA

Text copyright © 2010 by Dotti Enderle
All rights reserved
Printed in the United States of America
First edition

Library of Congress Cataloging-in-Publication Data

Enderle, Dotti, 1954–
Crosswire / by Dotti Enderle. — 1st ed.
p. cm.
Summary: When an 1883 drought drives free-range cattlemen to shred
Texas ranchers' barbed wire fences and steal water, thirteen-year-old
Jesse works hard to help while dealing with his father and brother's
falling-out and his own fear of guns. Includes bibliographical references.
ISBN 978-1-59078-751-9 (hardcover : alk. paper)
[1. Droughts—Fiction. 2. Fathers and sons—Fiction. 3. Brothers—
Fiction. 4. Robbers and outlaws—Fiction. 5. Courage—Fiction.
6. Ranch life—Texas—Fiction. 7. Texas—History—1846-1950—
Fiction.] I. Title.
PZ7.E69645Cro 2010
[Fic]—dc22

Barbed-wire images © Andy Brown: images from bigstockphoto.com

CALKINS CREEK
An Imprint of Boyds Mills Press, Inc.
815 Church Street
Honesdale, Pennsylvania 18431

10 9 8 7 6 5 4 3 2 1

I am a true Texan. A native Texan. It's part of my proud heritage. I guess I have my parents to thank for that. They were native Texans, too. And I grew up hearing their stories of hardship and happiness in the Texas plains.

Both of my parents were raised on cotton farms in the early 1900s. They continually reminded me how lucky I was that I never had to pick cotton. But I could still smell the cotton buds and feel the warm sun on my face as they recalled their times in the fields.

My parents were much more than the children of farmers. They contributed a small part in developing Texas. They helped shape its history.

I have my parents to thank for my love of Texas, Texas history, and my ability to weave that emotion into tales that honor spirited Texans just like them.

Texas history is rich with famous characters such as David Crockett, Jean Lafitte, and René-Robert Cavelier de La Salle. But there are many more who are not so well known—Jack C. Hays, Edward Burleson, and Dr. Charles Alderton.

Texans are making history every day. And just maybe, in the future, I can write about them, too.

—D. E.

ACKNOWLEDGMENTS

*I'd like to thank my first readers, Lenny and Adrienne Enderle,
Paeony Lewis, and Robin LaFevers.*

*And a special thank you to Tom Wancho of The Bob Bullock
Texas State History Museum for graciously reading the
manuscript for accuracy.*

Nature provides. There are crops for eating, horses for riding, and timber for shelter and heat. A season of rain keeps the cycle moving, and life flows along like a lazy stream. But nature can be unforgiving. When that happens all hell breaks loose—

as it did in Texas in 1883.

CHAPTER ONE

IN THE STINGING HEAT I HEARD HIM sneaking in through his bedroom window ... drunk again. From the sound of it, sloppy drunk. A loud thud, then some low chuckling. He'd fallen in. Drunk people are the world's worst at sneaking. I rolled over, trying to go back to sleep, but a loud crash sent me hopping out of bed.

"Ethan?" I whispered, opening my brother's bedroom door. He sat in the shadows, against the chest of drawers, one boot on, the other in his lap. His prize alligator boots. He was probably the only sixteen-year-old boy around to own any. And lordy, he loved strutting around town in them.

"Ethan." He just stared toward the corner, his eyes full of nothing. "Are you dead?" I asked, poking his arm. Kind of a fool question, but I've never poked a dead person before.

He lolled his head toward me and grinned. "Jesse. My favorite brother." His breath reeked of booze.

Nope, not dead, just drunker than a skunk. "I'm your *only* brother, stupid. And why'd you go and get drunk anyway? Papa's gonna kill you if he wakes up."

"Papa won't kill me. Not tonight." He dug into his breeches, bringing out a wad of money, a couple of poker chips, and the lining of his pocket. "I won, Jesse. I won!"

"Shhh!"

"My luck is changing." He tossed the money in the air. The poker chips hit the floor with a muffled clang. "One more night like tonight, and I can pay Papa back."

I knew he was just spitting out drunk talk. Papa would douse himself in kerosene and light a match before loaning Ethan any money. Of the two of us, Ethan had always been Papa's favorite. I was nothing but a shadow. Lately that had all changed. With Ethan's catting about at night, Papa had practically disowned him. 'Course that didn't promote me to favorite. Now Papa treated us both like hired help instead of his own flesh and blood.

"You're gonna pay Papa back for what?" I asked.

Ethan just waved his hand toward me and sat up, but only for a second. He dropped back, banging his head on the chest—hard.

"You're loco, you know that?" I reached down and tugged off the other alligator boot. He was lucky those boots hadn't gotten dulled and scuffed with his clumsiness. I clamped my hands onto his shoulders to help him to his bed. That's when I saw the blood, oozing down his forehead like molasses. "Did you get into a fight again?"

Reaching up, he touched it with his fingertip, then

chuckled some more. "Nope. That must be from when I fell and whacked it on this highboy." He rapped the chest with his knuckles like I couldn't tell which highboy he meant. The fool had no notion he was even hurt till I pointed it out.

I ain't ever been drunk myself, but I'm guessing it deadens every nerve in your body. Especially the nerves that cause pain. But that's probably why Ethan drank, to deaden the pain. Papa constantly had plans for Ethan, which mostly consisted of work. But Ethan wants to make his own plans. 'Course lately, his decision making wasn't too sharp.

I plopped him down onto his bed and grabbed a handkerchief from the top drawer. I couldn't risk going into the kitchen to pump water. There was some in the chamber pot under his bed, but I didn't want to dip my hands in that, even though I knew it hadn't been used since Mama cleaned it this morning. I placed the dry handkerchief on his forehead.

He grinned up at me, then clutched my shirt and tugged me toward him. Grabbing my neck, he squeezed me in a giant bear hug. "My baby brother."

"Stop it, Ethan, you dumb boozer." I'd seen him tipsy before. But never like this.

"I got an idea," he said. "Let's go fishing tomorrow. You and I ain't been fishing in a while."

Now that *was* drunk talk! "And just where are you going to find a fishing stream?" I said, pulling away from his grip. "You know this drought has everything as dry as buzzard food. You planning to buy a stream with that money you high-rolled from those cowhands tonight?"

He looked toward the ceiling, his mind a mile away. "I won. Just straight poker, but I won."

"Go to sleep." I left him to his drunken bliss and went back to my room. I needed to squeeze in a little more sleep before another hot July day drained me again. Farm chores are hard enough in fair weather, but working in this God-awful heat is like being whupped with a bag of hot cinders. And I wondered after tonight's shenanigans if Ethan would be able to pull his share.

The bed sheets were already wet from sweat, and I could hear my dog, Leather, settling down just below my window. His heavy panting had the rhythm of someone sawing through a thick board. As it slowed, so did my thoughts. I eased into a light sleep, wondering again if farming was all I'd ever be cut out for. Especially since I wasn't much cut out for it now. Ethan had dreams, and so did I. But sometimes dreams are just lies you make up to keep going day to day.

It seemed like I'd barely closed my eyes when Papa came pushing through my door. "Git up!"

I jerked awake from a dead sleep.

"And go wake up that brainless brother of yours. I don't have the stomach to look at him this morning."

I didn't much have the stomach for it either. Ethan's face was the same color as his scrambled eggs—even the whites of his eyes. He glanced down at his breakfast and heaved slightly, like he was about to retch. I wasn't sure what was nauseating him most, the looks of it or the smell. I just hoped he wasn't going to vomit right there at the table.

His hair was mussed and stringy, and hanging down on his forehead, mostly to cover that gash from the highboy. I could still see the cut though, and some jelly-looking bits stuck to it. But then, I already knew it was there. Anyone else probably couldn't tell what it was. His hair was doing the trick, but what kind of excuse would he come up with after pushing it back with his hat?

Papa kept his word. He never even took a glimpse in Ethan's direction. Instead he looked at Mama and spoke. "I'm thinking about digging a canal from the watering tank to the cotton field."

"A canal?" Mama said, pouring some strong black coffee into Ethan's cup.

Ethan rested his head on his hand, his elbow on the table. "Why? That'll just dry up the watering tank faster," he said, gazing toward Papa.

Papa's eyes sizzled like a fuse. He stabbed his ham with a fork. "You got a better plan for getting water to the cotton, smarty breeches?"

"No need," Ethan answered. "The cotton's dead. Take the losses and forget it. Better to have dead cotton than dead cows. You go digging a drainage canal, then what are the cattle going to drink?"

"I don't know," Papa said, his tone lethal. "Maybe you can bring them some whiskey from that dance hall you hang out in every danged night of the week!"

Not again.

Ethan stabbed his fork down, too, but it squeaked on the plate, and he winced at the noise.

I don't know why he can't just keep his mouth shut. Arguing with Papa is like digging through rock. Not that I was siding with Ethan. But the truth was, he was making sense. Dead cotton or dead cows? For someone who hated farming, Ethan knew more about it than Papa.

Mama spoke up quickly. "It's gonna rain soon. It will. I've been watching the ants. They know when rain's coming. All the signs are there. It's not like we haven't had droughts before."

"But not like this one," I said. I bet 1883 goes down in history as the worst.

Papa tore into a biscuit. "Well, until God takes the hint and it actually *does* rain, I think we need to consider digging that canal."

"Don't blaspheme, Tom," Mama said, her cheeks flushed.

Papa grunted. "Humph."

Ethan opened his mouth to say something else, but Mama jumped in again to avoid disaster. "I saw Mary Ann when I was in town yesterday. She said you haven't been round to see her in over a week. Aren't you still courting her?"

Ethan sighed. I think he'd rather fight with Papa than discuss his girlfriends. Especially the ones pushed on him by Mama. She always urged Ethan to take out the girls whose families tithed the biggest at church.

"Mary Ann was getting too serious," he muttered. "I thought maybe I should stay away for a bit."

"She was strangling him," I said, repeating what he'd told me a few nights ago. "He's too young to get married."

Ethan shot me a threatening look, then shoved me hard, nearly knocking me out of my chair.

"Well, I think she's a lovely girl," Mama continued. "I've invited her round for dinner after church this coming Sunday."

"I might not be here for dinner on Sunday," Ethan said. I could see him struggling between his hangover and an excuse.

"And besides," I said, wanting to pay him back for shoving me. "He's seeing Ruth now."

"Ruth?" Mama tilted her head and gazed at nothing. "I don't think I know Ruth."

"Uh—no—uh—nope." He sputtered the words like his tongue had quit working. Then he leaned toward me, and I could smell last night's rotgut sweating from his pores. "I'm gonna wallop you," he whispered.

"Before or after we go fishing?" I whispered back. I couldn't help but rub it in just to get back at him for all the trouble he caused with his drinking. And Mama would faint dead away if she knew Ruth was Catholic. Having that leverage over him could come in handy when he tried passing his share of chores over to me because of his hangover.

Papa drained his coffee cup and stood up. "Enough fool talk. No girl in her right mind would want a sot like him anyway. Come on, let's ride out to the tank."

Old Leather Dog was waiting on the back porch. There were flies buzzing round him, and I couldn't help but think

that had to be torture for a dog with no hair. "Come on, boy."
He trotted behind me as Ethan and I went out to the barn to
fetch our horses.

"Not feeling so lucky this morning, huh?" I had to tease.
Maybe he'd learned his lesson this time.

Ethan trudged along. "I feel like I've been mule-kicked
right in the gut."

I opened the barn door since he didn't look like he had
the strength. "How did you get that money ... really?"

"Did I tell you I won it at poker?"

"Yep."

He nodded. "I won it at poker." He looked away when
he said it, and with Ethan, that meant there was more to
the story.

Papa came in right then and untied his horse. We quickly
hushed, and went about untying our own. "No foolishness,
you hear me?" Papa slid the shotgun into his saddle holster. He
tossed Ethan's rifle to him.

Papa always brought the guns when we rode out to the
back pasture. We'd had some wild boars from time to time.
I didn't have a gun. 'Course I'd rather try to outrun a boar
than fire a gun any day. But I kept that to myself as much as
possible. A thirteen-year-old boy who doesn't hunt and shoot
is about as disappointing as a son who drinks and gambles.

We took out across the dust and dried grass. Leather
galloped behind us, white slobber drooling from his jowls. The
sun was barely up, but the day was already frying everything
in sight. Papa rode several paces ahead, and when we reached
the back pasture, he pulled on the reins, coming to a sudden

halt. "Dammit!" he shouted, snatching off his hat and throwing it to the ground.

I looked down at the tank. Hoof prints. It had been trampled. And then I saw the back fence. That's how they'd gotten in. The barbed wire had been cut and pulled back.

Papa gritted his teeth, cussing under his breath.

"It was only a matter of time," Ethan said. "We're probably the only farm around that hadn't been cut."

Ethan was right. The fence-cutters were getting desperate. They'd cut any fence they could to water their cattle.

I glanced toward the oak tree that stood near the crosswire. A shiver spurred me, and my veins felt like acid. 'Cause someone had hung a long strand of barbed wire from a limb … shaped into a hangman's noose.

CHAPTER TWO

PAPA SET US TO MENDING THE FENCE, then headed off to tend the cows. I strung the barbed wire while Ethan hammered. From the grimace on his face, every nail he pounded hammered in his brain, too. I bet hangovers are worse than hornet stings.

Ethan didn't let it stop him, though. He was a good worker. He used to whistle through every chore, but lately there's just not enough spit in this hellish heat to whistle for a dog.

Leather had found a bare spot under the oak and stretched out in the shade. He was lying on his back, belly up. The only part of him that moved was his eyes, watching Ethan and me repair the fence.

We worked in silence for the most part, until Ethan took a break. "You gotta admire the fence-cutters," he said after a big swallow of water.

"What?" I couldn't have heard him right. "You're taking their side?"

"Naw," he said, taking another swig from the canteen. "A man has a right to fence what's his. But think about it. The fence-cutters are free. They believe in the open range. And they'll do whatever they have to just to water their stock."

"And we'll do whatever we have to just to protect ours," I said.

"Rebuilding a fence? Shoot. Mending a fence doesn't hold the same meaning as cutting one. These men are like the famous outlaws. They take what the land has to offer."

"Well, first of all," I pointed out, "they're not *like* outlaws, they *are* outlaws. And second, the land isn't offering much for the taking this year. When they cut our fence, they're stealing water … our water."

"On the other hand, I think they did us a favor." He winked.

"You're loco," I said, unwinding more barb.

He gave me a crooked grin. "Would you rather be mending a fence or digging a drainage ditch to the cotton?"

Gotta hand it to him. He had a point.

Ethan reached down for one of the fallen fence posts. He rolled it aside, then froze. Dead still. He didn't even blink. That's when I heard it. Just a foot away was the biggest rattler I believe I'd ever seen. My mouth went dry. Ethan stayed calm. One false move and we'd be digging his grave.

Leather Dog slinked over, rolling a menacing growl.

"Jesse," Ethan whispered, staring the snake down. "Quick. Get my rifle."

I tiptoed, but I hurried. As I slipped it out of his saddle pack, I wondered how in tarnation I was going to hand it to him without putting myself in danger. "Here it is," I whispered.

He never looked up. "Kill it."

"What?" I could see sweat pouring from his brow. The dried blood oozed with it, looking like mud. It dripped into his eyes, but he still didn't blink. "Now, Jesse."

I looked at the gun, then the snake. It was coiled in a tight circle, staring up at Ethan—a showdown between man and serpent. It rattled again and I jumped. Leather's growl grew louder.

"I'm gonna be dead in about two seconds if you don't kill this thing now!"

I fidgeted with the rifle, laid it down, then grabbed the posthole digger.

Ethan's eyes had to be stinging. His composure failed when I put the gun down, and I could see him start to shake. "Are you crazy?" he whispered, his voice like sand.

Yeah, I guess I am. Just as the snake decided to strike, I jabbed it with the posthole digger, cutting it into three bloody pieces.

"You gall-dang fool!" Ethan screamed, pushing me so hard I nearly fell into the watering tank. "I told you to shoot it!"

"No you didn't. You told me to kill it."

"Why do you think I asked you to get the rifle?" He danced around, probably letting go of all that bottled up fear.

"I killed it, okay?"

He wiped his face on his sleeve, and for the first time I could see the tears mixed in with the sweat. "Papa would throw nineteen fits if he'd seen that. Are you ever going to get over your fear of guns?"

"Are you ever going to give up drinking and gambling?"

"That ain't the same thing!" he fumed. His ears were turning a deeper red, and I could see extra scarlet on his cheeks that didn't come from the sun. "You shoulda shot it."

"And what if I'd missed?" I asked him.

He let out a hopeless sigh, shaking his head. "Jesse, what happened to Smokey wouldn't happen again in a million years."

Yep, that'd been pounded into my head a hundred times since the day Smokey died. But somehow my brain wasn't getting the message. He'd been the best farm dog in Texas until he got in the way of my bullet. Nope, unlike Ethan, I wasn't a gambler, and I couldn't bring myself to chance it, even with those odds.

He doused his head with some water from the canteen, then sucked in some loud deep breaths. He sat there for a full minute or more.

Of course I didn't expect Ethan to thank me. If the predicament had been reversed, Ethan would have blasted that rattler to a holy hell, then hugged me for not getting bit. But it's over, and I couldn't change it if I wanted to. I couldn't. He'll just keep on thinking I'm a yellow-belly. But I've been marked a coward for a while now, and that ain't going to change anytime soon. I'll just keep playing it safe.

I watched him shake off his last jittery nerves then face me. "This fence ain't gonna mend itself," he said. And we didn't talk again until it was done.

Mending a fence was just one extra task. We still had all of our other chores left to do. With the crops failing, Papa couldn't afford the sharecroppers. Even if he could, Mama teases that he's a penny-pinching old miser anyway. She's right, although I leave that joking to her. Get Papa riled up too much, and he's keen to taking the strap to us.

As I worked, I imagined chilly things. Like a dip in a crystal blue lake, or the foamy waves of the Gulf. But my imagination just wasn't as strong as the sun. And neither was my hat. A few times I thought I might drop from brain scorch, but sitting in a shady spot with my head between my knees always brought some sense back into me. I decided I'd say extra prayers next Sunday at church. If hell was hotter than this, I most definitely wanted to stay out.

The devil sun eventually set, and we sat out on the porch to catch a breeze. Mama did some mending while Papa just rocked and smoked his pipe. I used a piece of frayed rope to play tug-o-war with Leather.

Ethan came out on the porch, but he didn't sit down. "Think those scoundrels will be back tonight with the wire cutters?" he asked Papa.

Papa shook his head. "Ain't nobody that blame stupid. I'm guessing they'll strike somewhere else."

"'Course, they could figure that you wouldn't be expecting 'em, and come straight back here. You know, trying to outsmart you."

Papa turned and looked at him. "They're a bunch of dang cowards and fools, son. They ain't got enough brains to outsmart their own horses." He kept staring at Ethan like something was wrong. "What you all duded up about?"

I looked up at him, too. Papa was right. Ethan was wearing a clean shirt and trousers, and his hair was slicked back with tonic oil.

"I'm going out," Ethan said, trying to sound brave, but failing.

Papa narrowed his eyes. "Where?"

Mama sure could smell trouble in a hurry. "I do hope you're going to see Mary Ann. You look so handsome." She smiled at him, but I could see her jaws were clenched.

"Don't start with that, Mama," Ethan said, opening the screen door. "I won't be too late tonight."

"So then I guess you're going to see Ruth." I shouted it a little too loud, wanting to see his reaction before he disappeared back into the house. I had to get in my dig. It was my way of reminding Ethan that I still had that leverage. And I guess I sort of resented that he got to hang around town while I was stuck out here with just Mama and Papa and Old Leather Dog for company.

"Ain't none of your business," he said, his eyes like gunpowder.

"Don't you like her?" I teased. "She's got that long dark hair. Ruby lips." I accompanied those last words with some kissy noises. "And eyes as crossed as a hobo's."

"That's it," he said, hurrying across the porch and grabbing my neck in the crook of his arm. "I'm gonna knuckle you." I got a good sniff of the toilet water he'd sprinkled on.

"Cut it out!" Papa hollered. Ethan did.

"You should bring Ruth around to meet us," Mama said. "Or have we already met? I don't recall any of the young ladies at church called Ruth."

You wouldn't, I thought. *Not at the Baptist church.* Ethan gave me a gaze that said, *You tell and I'll kill you.*

"I won't be out late," he repeated.

Just as he was heading in, I called, "You sure do stink pretty!"

He stuck his head back out the door and sneered.

I'm not sure what time it was that night when I had to visit the privy. I had too much business for the chamber pot. Leather followed me to the outhouse and back, but stopped just before we reached the back door. His ears perked, and he let loose a low rumbling growl. His attention was on something way out in the back pasture. He took out, racing like the wind and barking like a dog gone mad. I couldn't see what was out there. It was too far away, and the night too dark. But whatever it was, it was happening far off, probably near the crosswire again.

"Leather!" I called in a loud whisper. I'd probably gone mad, too, thinking he could even hear me. His barking faded through the pasture as he put some distance between us.

Who was out there? I couldn't hear a thing. I was wishing I had the listening abilities of a dog 'cause something had put Leather into action.

I waited for a second, worrying. Were they there now— sneaking along the back pasture clipping our fence? And what would they do if Leather came up on them? My stomach felt as prickly as a porcupine. Surely they wouldn't hurt a dog.

I figured I could slip my horse out of the barn and ride out to check. But what would I do if they were there? Blasted fences! I didn't give a hoot about wire and wood. I only cared about Leather. I had to get my dog back.

I went back inside for my pants and boots, trying not to make a ruckus that woke everyone. My stomach felt like Mama's butter churn, pumping bile into my throat. Maybe I should wake Papa? But then, what if it turned out to be nothing? Knowing the right thing to do just gets too tricky at times.

I finished buttoning my shirt and headed out to the barn. There was no chickening out. I *had* to get my dog. I'd barely lifted my saddle when the door creaked open.

"Jesse?"

Ethan walked his horse in, and even in the dead of night, I could see the questions on his face.

"Leather Dog ran off," I told him. "I think the fence-cutters are back."

"And you're going out to go stop them?" he asked.

"I just need to round up Leather, that's all. I don't give a plug nickel about the fence."

Which was true. Course I might be singing a different tune if I'm stuck mending it again.

Ethan stomped by me, leading his horse into his stall. "Don't be a fool, Jesse. Just get your tail-end back to bed."

"Not till I know Leather's all right."

He closed the stall gate, shaking his head. I hated the way he dismissed me and any notion I had.

"Look," he said, like he was pointing out something obvious. "These men just want to water their cows and horses. They're not gonna hurt a dog—even an ugly dog like Leather."

Ethan walked toward me, steady and straight. He must've been with Ruth tonight because I didn't smell a single whiff of whiskey on his breath. And it seemed too early for gambling hours to end.

"You better be right," I told him, putting my saddle back.

He clapped his hand hard to my shoulder and led me out of the barn. "I'm always right," he said.

Turns out, he was wrong.

CHAPTER THREE

MAMA SHOOK ME, WHISPERING, "Get up, Jesse. Something's wrong with your dog."

I jumped out of bed, my bare feet hitting the floor hard. Racing past her, I ran to the back porch. Leather was lying there in his usual spot, panting with pain. Then I saw the bloody spots around his neck. The skin was ripped with uneven gashes, like he'd been given some kind of thorny collar. Mama came out with a bottle of ointment and rags.

The day hadn't broke yet, but there was a hint of the sun in the east. Mama's egg basket sat empty, like she'd been interrupted from going to the hen house. She squatted down next to me and began doctoring Leather's neck.

Leather's breathing eased as Mama and I went to work trying to seal the wounds. "What did this?" I asked.

Mama nodded toward the ground. "I found him with this around his neck."

I saw it. A long string of barbed wire. New wire. Leather *had* caught wind of those fence-cutting scoundrels last night, and they'd managed to hush him up in the cruelest way. I'm just glad Mama had removed the barbs from Leather before waking me up. I don't think I could've took it. I sure wish Ethan could have seen him that way though. It'd shut him up forever about being right. And maybe he wouldn't admire the fence-cutters anymore. I could kick myself in the head for not doing something last night when I'd had the chance.

"It was a downright vicious act," Mama said, tying a damp towel around Leather's neck. "After all the work you did healing this poor dog from that bout of mange. And he's a good dog. He didn't deserve that cruel trick."

I rubbed his head and scratched his ears. "I just wish his hair had grown back … to protect him."

"You did a good job taking care of him, Jesse. He's alive because of you. You'll see him through this, too."

I leaned over and laid my head on top of Leather's. It was the only way I could give him a hug without upsetting the wounds on his neck. My heart ached. He must have sensed my feelings, because he turned his head and licked my face. "Good boy," I said while he gave my chin a good cleaning.

Mama sat back and straightened her apron. She brushed my hair away from my forehead and grinned. "Ethan came in early last night."

"I reckon he did," I said.

"You think he went to see that girl? Ruth?" She smiled innocently, but I knew when I was cornered.

"Maybe." I kept petting Leather.

"Have you met her, Jesse?"

"Once. A couple of weeks ago when I went into town with Ethan. We ran into her at the store."

Mama nodded and reached for the egg basket. I thought I was off the hook, but she fidgeted with it, not making any effort to get up. "Is she pretty?"

"I reckon." I thought about her dark hair pulled back with a ribbon. Her skin like honey glaze. I think she's part Mexican. Of course I knew better than to say too much.

"Is she new in town?" Mama coaxed.

"Maybe." She probably wasn't, but I was hoping the less I answered, the less she'd ask.

"I wonder why she's never at church on Sundays?"

"Maybe she's a Methodist." I looked away 'cause I was afraid she'd see the truth in my eyes.

"I bet that's it," she said, getting up and hooking the basket on her arm. "She's probably new in town, and her family are Methodists." Mama went off down the steps, seeming satisfied with that.

I was just happy the questions had ended. With Ethan drinking, gambling, and seeing a Catholic girl, I figured he was building his own sticky fence with Mama and Papa. And it sure wasn't up to me to cut it.

When Ethan saw what had happened to Leather Dog, he squawked like a mad rooster. "That's it! Who do they think they are?" He paced back and forth, his face tight with anger. "I'm hiding out tonight to see if I can catch 'em."

"You ain't doing no such thing," Papa said, putting on his hat.

"But they can't get away with this!"

"They already have," Papa said. "Fussing ain't gonna change it."

I couldn't believe it. Why wasn't Papa roaring mad himself? Did he have something up his sleeve?

"I can't change it, but I can sure kick their sorry behinds for it!" Ethan threatened.

I waited. Ethan owed me an apology, or he could at least admit he was wrong. If only he hadn't talked me out of going out there … bringing Leather back before they'd rigged their own way to quiet his barking.

Papa motioned for us to head out. "Stop your agitating and save that energy for mending the fence," he said.

Mend it again? That sure seemed like a fool thing to do. What if they outsmart Papa and come back again tonight … and tomorrow night … and the next? As long as we have water and the sky doesn't, there's no telling how many times they'll cut our fence. It's a shame that rattlesnake hadn't been sitting there waiting for *them*.

Leather didn't follow us this time. He stayed on the porch, his head resting on his paws. I guess dogs have enough sense to take it easy when they're hurt. His eyes were alert, so I knew he'd pull through this.

My jaws dropped when we reached the back fence. Those fence-cutters must have been fuming mad that we rebuilt it. They didn't just cut it, they hacked it to hell. Barbed wire scattered everywhere. They'd cut yards of it, from the crosswire to the cotton field. And not only that, they'd chopped up a bunch of the fence posts with an axe.

We didn't have enough materials to rebuild it that morning. We'd have to get supplies from town. Papa stared, not bothering to get off his horse. He turned and looked at Ethan and me. The devil sang in his eyes, and he meant for someone to burn.

CHAPTER FOUR

PAPA HATED THE FENCE-CUTTERS, and now Ethan did, too. So did I … I guess. I hated them for what they did to Old Leather Dog, but hate is a funny thing. It's hard to focus your hate when you don't know exactly who it is you're hating. None of us knew who the fence-cutters were. Just faceless enemies, destroying everything we had—our fence, our water, our dog. I wanted to hate them with a passion. But until I saw them, until I knew exactly who was doing this to us, I had to hate blindly.

It made me think of Papa and religion. Mama always wanted him to be a good Baptist like her, but Papa wasn't a religious man, and he didn't make no bones about it. "If I can't see it, touch it, taste it, hear it, or smell it," he'd say, "it just don't exist." But I knew dang well the fence-cutters existed. So I just directed all that hate the same way I'd direct my prayers to an invisible God. Praying for them to stop would probably have been better than trying to hate them, but people can't always do the right thing—the Christian thing. So no matter what the good book says, I had to do the *human* thing.

Papa had gone into town alone and was late showing up for dinner. Our stomachs were growling like Old Leather Dog by the time he got home. He'd brought back the fence-mending supplies and not much else. I thought for sure he'd be full of conversation about things going on in town or the business of other ranchers. But he chewed his food like he was contemplatin' every bite, without hardly uttering a word.

We spent the rest of the evening as silent as a graveyard, and after Mama and Papa had gone to bed, I sat on the porch, my brain too wound up to sleep. My mind kept replaying the night before, and all the things I could've done different. Leather was still feeling peaked from his wounds. I'd doctored them several times, until Mama told me not to use up all the ointment. But Leather couldn't reach his neck to lick it clean, and that's how dogs heal themselves. I had to do what I could.

The pasture was lit with lightning bugs, and at the band of the horizon, you couldn't tell the fireflies from the stars. It was a sight that put me and Leather Dog both at ease. Ethan came out on the back porch and sat on the steps.

"I thought you were asleep," I said, petting Leather's belly.

"Naw, I'm too much of a night owl. I'm going out directly."

I couldn't believe he'd do this. There were enough problems now without him creating new ones.

"Anyway," he kept on, "I thought you might want to come with me." He turned and grinned and I knew he meant it.

"To see Ruth? Three's a crowd, ain't it?""

"Not seeing Ruth," he said, leaning his elbows on his knees and looking up at the sky. "I'm heading for the saloon. You wanna come?"

I couldn't believe he was even asking me. "Papa would wring my neck if— "

"Papa won't know," Ethan argued.

"You can't be sure," I said.

"I can hear him snoring all the way out here! Come on, Jesse, go with me."

I thought hard on it. I'd been stuck out here for a couple of weeks, and those stars were lighting a trail. But sneaking out? "Why should I trust you?" I asked him. "You proved last night you ain't always right."

He looked down at his boots and nodded. "I admit it. And I'm really sorry Leather got hurt. But you could lock him in the barn tonight. He'd be safe there."

He'd be safe, but what about me? I looked toward the back door like Papa might walk out anytime, just knowing we were up to something. It didn't feel right. "Why would I want to go to a saloon to watch a bunch of dusty old cowboys picking their teeth and rustling cards anyway?"

"Have you ever been inside a saloon before?" Ethan asked me.

"Of course I ain't." Could it really be all that great? I admit, I was curious why Ethan liked spending so many nights there. But still, it'd break Mama's heart, and I hate to think what Papa would do to me. "I better stay here with Leather," I said.

Ethan shook his head. "Look at him, Jesse. He's fine. All

them cuts are already scabbing over. His eyes are clear, his tail is wagging."

"It's late." I was stumbling for an excuse, but I knew Ethan well enough to know he never accepted anybody's excuses. Nobody's.

"Late is the best time to go to a saloon," he told me. "Come on, we won't stay out too long. I need to win some more money, and you can be there to stop me if I start losing."

That seemed the most logical reason to go. If I could keep Ethan from doing something fool-headed like gambling away money he didn't have, it might be worth the risk.

He reached over and nudged me. "Come on, little brother. It's Friday night. There'll be a good crowd. We'll have a good time. And I want to make it up to you about last night."

I slowly picked myself up from the porch. We could be to the saloon and back in the time it would take me to talk Ethan out of making me go. "Just swear to me that Mama and Papa won't find out about this."

Ethan grinned like a possum. "I swear."

I paused and gave him a doubtful look. "Are you right this time?"

His grin turned devilish. "Absolutely."

We were about a quarter mile from the farm when Ethan and I kicked our horses into a gallop. Their hooves clicked a soft rhythm on the hard packed dirt. The crickets were especially loud, and the night seemed darker than most. We didn't slow down until the road widened near town.

Everything was quiet and dark except for the lanterns glowing in front of the Wild Horse Saloon. Light poured from the windows, and you could hear the music before you even got anywhere near Main Street. It was the only signs of life after ten o'clock at night.

We rode up, pretty as you please, and tied our horses at the hitching post. I stayed behind Ethan as he poked out his chest and swung the doors open like he owned the place. Just before I went in, I stumbled on a dark lump gathered up next to the doors. Two bright eyes shined up at me.

"Pud Taylor! What you doing here?" Pud was just a little whipper, the son of one of the sharecroppers who used to help us pick cotton. Of course that was when there was plenty of cotton to pick and to share.

"What're you doing here, Jesse?"

I was wondering the same thing myself. "I'm thirteen years old. I can come here if I want. But look at you. Shouldn't you still be tied to your mama's apron strings?" I had no idea how old Pud was, but if I had to guess I'd say he wasn't any more than eight or nine.

"I come here a lot," Pud said. "I like to sit out here and listen to the piano." He pronounced it pie-annie. "And besides, when some of the men win at poker, they come out feeling rich and hand me a coin or two. If they're stinking drunk, they drop coins on the ground as they stumble off."

I nodded at Pud, admiring his gumption. "Beats picking cotton," I said.

Pud nodded back. "Amen to that."

Ethan stuck his head out. "Come on, Jesse."

Inside, a smoke-gray haze hung in the air. We cut through it to the bar. Ethan put his foot on the boot railing and leaned against the polished cherry wood. He seemed to only care about getting something to drink. I soon had a different notion. I couldn't take my eyes off the picture that hung up over the bottles of booze. It was a portrait of a plump woman on a gold swing, leaning back with a rose clenched in her mouth. She wasn't necessarily beautiful or anything, but she was as bare as a newborn baby. She was swinging upward, and her hair flowed behind her. Her bosoms were large, and her rump hung over the back of the swing. I don't know why anyone would want to swing in the altogether with a rose in her mouth, much less pose for a portrait like that, but by gosh, I wasn't complaining. That picture must have been really old though, because the swing was hanging from an apple tree, and those apples were rusty brown and didn't look fit to eat.

"Just a beer for me," Ethan said, flipping a coin at the barkeeper. "And bring my brother here a shot of the hard stuff."

The barkeep laughed as he caught the coin in midair. So did some men sitting at the table next to us. "You in tonight, Ethan?" one of them asked. He was a stranger to me, although I recognized a couple of the cowhands sitting there with him. Dale Finch and Buster Caulden, both looking dirty and rough.

"Gotta pay off my debts, Billy," Ethan said, dragging a chair out with the toe of his boot. He slid into it, then pulled a wad of money from his pocket. I swear it was a heck of a lot more than he had a few nights ago. I couldn't imagine where he got it.

"Grab a chair from that table, Jesse," he said, motioning toward it.

I went over to the table and reached for the chair. The man next to it propped his feet up on it and crossed them before I could get it away. "Where's your manners, Jesse?" he said while biting the mushy stub of a cigar.

I didn't really know the man, and I surely didn't know how he knew my name, but I figured I'd better say please. Ethan cut in before the word came out of my mouth. "Cut it out, Earnest! Let him have the chair."

Earnest slid his feet off the chair, then kicked it hard, nearly knocking me down. A roar of laughter came up from half the room. I knew then that I didn't belong here. I couldn't imagine why Ethan wanted me to come.

Since I wasn't playing poker, I couldn't sit up at the table. I sat back just behind Ethan instead. "Hope your brother's got a poker face," Buster said to Ethan. "Or else we'll be cleaning you out tonight."

Ethan frowned. "Scoot over some, Jesse, and don't be looking at my cards."

Just then a woman came up to the table all dressed in purple satin and green ribbons. She was all frilly from head to foot, and wore more paint on her face than a wild Injun. Her skirt was gathered up on one side, and pinned that way with a fancy brooch. I could see her leg all the way up past her knee. She plopped a beer down in front of Ethan. Some of the foam spilled over and ran down the side.

"And for Jesse, I brought the finest whiskey." She sat a glass in front of me, filled with sarsaparilla. This brought some chuckles from the men at the table. But to make matters worse, she added, "Oh, I almost forgot," then dropped a long-stem cherry into it. Half the room roared with laughter again. I was about ready to crawl underneath that table, or go sit out front with Pud. Was this why Ethan wanted me here? So his friends could have someone to pick on? I shrugged it off, figuring they'd get used to me soon enough and the teasing would wear thin. But Ethan reached into my sarsaparilla and pulled the cherry out. "Stop picking on my little brother." He slung the cherry at Buster who snatched it in the air, and popped it into his mouth, stem and all.

"Hey, darlin'," the saloon lady said, leaning toward Ethan and putting her foot up on the edge of his chair.

"Hi, Mabel." Ethan smiled and ran his hand up her calf. I couldn't believe what I was seeing! His hand crept up past her knee, and I could see her lacy garter. My face caught fire from embarrassment, and I wanted to look away, but it was just too hard not to look. It's the only time I'd seen up the dress of a girl who wasn't sporting a pair of ruffled bloomers. I didn't turn away. If she was letting all these cowboys look, then there was no reason I couldn't look, too.

"How 'bout a date, sweetie?" she asked him.

"I can't afford to take you out, Mabel. I hear you want men to buy you diamonds and furs."

"I'll settle for a juicy steak and a goodnight kiss," Mabel said.

"I'll tell you what. You send me some winning luck tonight, and I'll buy you the whole cow."

Mabel leaned in closer, her red lips nearly touching his. "And if you don't win, maybe I can have a date with your little brother here."

That set them all to laughing again. "Stop it," Ethan said, pushing her away.

"I'll have a date with you, Mabel," Buster yelled out.

Mabel curled her lip at him. "You need a date with a bar of soap."

Laughter rose up again, and for once, thank goodness, the joke wasn't on me.

Ethan's mind was on his poker game and mine was on the saloon. Through the cigar fog I could see the room was mostly filled with cowhands, but back in the far corner, there sat a few familiar faces. The more well-known ranchers in town had their own poker game going at a private table. My eyes slowly moved back around to get another glimpse of that lady on the swing, but someone had sat down at the bar between me and the portrait. An odd sort of stranger. He was tall and thin, his shirt sleeves rolled up to his elbows. He threw back a shot of whiskey, then turned around toward us. His hat was tilted back, and his bushy mustache covered his top lip. It was obvious he'd just rode in, and from the looks of him it'd been a hard ride. He scratched his square jaw and nodded at me. I looked away. But not before noticing his sharp blue eyes. I got a funny feeling about him.

The stranger stayed right there on that barstool for the next couple of hours. I sat in my spot, trying to stay awake while Ethan, one hand after another, lost all those winnings from the other night. I tried to warn him a time or two, but he got downright agitated. "I brought you here to have a good time," he told me, "not spoil my night."

'Course I couldn't help but think he'd just piddled it all away, and once he was completely out of the game, he turned madder than a rabid coon. I just kept my mouth shut as we got up to leave.

"This doesn't settle the whole debt," Dale said, gripping Ethan's arm as we got up to leave.

"Yep," Buster bellowed, standing up. "If you really want to settle, where's them alligator boots you're usually wearin'?" He craned his neck under the table to look at Ethan's feet. But Ethan hadn't worn them tonight. Probably for this reason.

"I'll pay you both back!" Ethan barked, kicking his chair to the side. "And you ain't touching my alligator boots!" His eyes were narrowed and tense as he pointed a finger at Buster. I sure wasn't looking forward to the ride back home.

"You win anything?" Pud asked Ethan as we pushed through the swinging doors.

"Go to hell!" Ethan answered.

"Just askin'," Pud said.

Relief flooded me once we were out of there. I'll take the dusty night air over choking cigar smoke any day. We rode off, worry being the only thing keeping me awake. What had gotten into Ethan? Was he really in a heap of debt? The looks in those gamblers' eyes told me we'd have a lot more to deal with than a drought.

CHAPTER FIVE

THOSE FIVE MILES BACK TO THE FARM prickled my hide, 'cause Ethan kicked up a fuss the whole way, most of it a bunch of rambling I couldn't make out. I just ignored him, more worried about what trouble I'd be in if Mama or Papa had woke up and looked in my room. Ethan didn't care. He was so fiery mad, the whole world could wake up and pitch a fit. He'd never notice. But when we finally reached the road to our house, Ethan's voice dropped to a whisper like Papa might actually hear him from that far away. "I'll take the horses to the barn, Jesse. You slip in through your bedroom window."

"You don't think I'll get caught?"

Ethan shook his head. "You know Papa sleeps like a bear in hibernation. Not much will wake him up."

Just before we split paths, I whispered, "Ethan, why'd you want me there with you tonight?"

The anger dissolved from his face. "You don't know?"

I shook my head because truthfully, I didn't. It was obvious that he hadn't really wanted me to stop him from losing all his money. So maybe he thought my being there would keep those roughnecks from ripping him apart in payment for what he owed them. Or maybe he really did want me there.

He just gave me that crooked grin of his and led our horses away.

I didn't believe Papa was really that heavy of a sleeper, but I did what Ethan said. As I got to my window, Leather came trouncing around the corner, all fired up. "It's just me," I said as soft as I could. I tried to pet him, but he wouldn't settle down. He was always good at sensing trouble, but tonight he wasn't barking, just acting agitated. "It's all right." I looked around thinking maybe the fence-cutters had come back. But why? We hadn't repaired the fence, and they could herd their stock right up to our watering tank without a bit of fuss.

I crawled in through the window as hushed as I could, and was proud of how quiet I'd done it. A shadow could make more noise. I got undressed and into bed, thinking how tired I'd be in a few hours when Papa came to wake me up. I'd just settled into my pillow when I heard Ethan coming in the back door through the kitchen. He was quiet, too. But seconds later I heard, "You lousy no-good scoundrel!" Then the sound of fist on flesh. Mama screamed while Papa cussed to high heaven. Leather started barking and scratching to get in.

I flew out of bed and peeked around into the kitchen. The room was lit by a dim kerosene lamp, but I could still see what had happened. Ethan was on the floor with a bloody nose. Mama was on her knees next to him, crying hysterically and wiping his face with her nightgown. He gently pushed her aside and stood up, his chest poking out toward Papa. "That's all I am to you now. All I'll ever be. A no-good scoundrel!"

Papa held up the strongbox where he kept the family savings locked away. It was as empty as the creek beds. "I've told you boys all your life that I don't allow no thieves in my house!" Papa hauled off and backhanded him this time. I saw the sweat sling off Ethan's forehead as his face twisted in pain.

Leather Dog went wild again, growling this time.

"Stop it, Tom!" Mama cried. "Stop it now!"

Papa just gazed at Ethan with the devil's stare.

"Please!" Mama screamed, her hands shaking from fear.

I was quaking all over, too. But Papa would have none of Mama's begging. "Get back in the bedroom, Cora. This is between the boy and me."

I'd never heard him call Ethan "the boy." He'd called me that a few times, mostly when I did something to disappoint him. Until recently, Ethan had been the favorite in Papa's eyes. He'd really messed up this time.

Mama scurried over to where I stood on the other side of the doorway. She fell against me, hugging me like I was the one getting beat up instead of Ethan. She cried enough tears to water the cattle.

I held onto her, trying to be strong. I never was any good at that. I had tears streaming down my face, mostly from fear.

"What'd you do with all my money!" Papa hollered. "You gamble it away?"

He'd barely got those words out when Ethan doubled his fist and struck Papa in the jaw. Papa stumbled back, crashing against the cookstove. "You sorry maggot! You'd hit your own father?" Papa's face was the color of blood. He grabbed the griddle off the stove and headed toward Ethan.

"No!" Mama screamed, her shout ringing in my ear. "Don't hurt my little boy!"

She tore away from me and ran between Papa and Ethan. Papa shoved her aside, but not before Ethan reached for the cutting board and grabbed a butcher knife.

"You want to punish me, old man?" he said, blood and tears streaking to his chin. "You want to teach me a lesson? Too late!" He held the knife not two feet from Papa's throat, and Papa stood dead still, looking at the blade. "This is what you taught me! You taught me that no matter how hard you work in life it ain't never enough! Never! Jesse and I missed half our schooling because you thought we'd be better served breaking our backs for you! You want to teach me a lesson? Teach me now. Teach me that there ain't nothing better outside of this house ... this farm. Teach me that I won't do better in St. Louis or New Orleans. I'm listening, Papa! Teach me that!"

Papa dropped the griddle and shuffled over to the back door. "Get out of my house," he said, opening it wide.

"No! No!" Mama cried, running to Ethan and holding him back. "Tom, have you lost your mind? He's just a boy—just sixteen. Didn't you ever go out sowing your wild oats at that age? Tom!"

"I didn't rob from my own father," he said calmly, his eyes and voice demanding. "Get out, Ethan. Don't ever come back to this house again."

Ethan pulled Mama's grip from his arm and stomped to

the door. He stared Papa straight in the eyes. "Don't think you threw me out, you old geezer. I'm leaving on my own."

"Not quick enough," Papa said, slamming the door hard.

I heard Leather whimper and follow Ethan off the back porch.

Papa turned and looked at each of us, first me, then Mama. His eyes were full of hurt, but he kept his gaze steady. "The boy is dead, Cora," he said, like it was really true.

"No," Mama whispered. "No, Tom."

"He's dead to me ... and to you. And you too, Jesse. I've always said I wouldn't house no thieves. He's good and dead now, and neither one of you are to mention his name again, you understand me? Ever!"

He stomped past me and down the hall. Mama collapsed to her knees, praying to God and Jesus and whoever else up there she thought could help. I went over and took her in my arms, as shaky as they were.

"He'll come around in a few days, Mama. You'll see. He won't hold a grudge on Ethan."

Mama looked up at me, her blue eyes pale and weak. "I've been married to that man for eighteen years, Jesse. He means it. We won't ever see Ethan again."

I felt a stabbing in my heart when she said that. I wanted to chase after Ethan right then. Thank him for taking me to the saloon with him tonight. Tell him I was sorry for teasing him so much. I wanted to remind him of all the good times we'd had when we were little, hiding in the cornfield, swimming in the watering tank, and picnicking under the old oak by the crosswire. I wanted to say so much. All the things that people want to say to their brothers when they really die.

I helped Mama to her room, but she didn't want to go in. Finally, she opened the door. Papa was already in bed.

"Good night, son," she said, taking my face in her hands and kissing my cheek. She seemed to wilt away as she closed the door.

I went back to my room and looked out the window to see if I could spot Ethan anywhere around, even though I knew it was a hopeless thing to do. Leather had settled in the dirt just below my windowsill. His eyes were keen, looking around as though to protect me.

I gazed out at the still night, knowing I wouldn't be getting much sleep. My brother was gone. *Gone.* And worst of all, I never got to say goodbye.

CHAPTER SIX

"**GET UP, JESSE," PAPA SAID,** shaking my bed. "Lots of work to do."

I tried to open my eyes, but they felt gritty and burnt. I rubbed them with my fists and tried again. It was still black as pitch outside, and I was guessing it couldn't be more than four-thirty in the morning. I didn't get to sleep until after two.

I managed to pull myself up out of bed, even though my heart still sagged from what'd happened just a few hours before. Ethan would come back. He had to come back. It was only a matter of when. But until then, Papa had to rely on me. And that's a big responsibility. How many more ways could I disappoint him?

I scuffled into the kitchen. No breakfast. Papa had boiled some coffee on the stove. I poured a cup, but it bit my tongue and tasted bitter going down. I knew better than ask where Mama was. She had to be asleep ... or still heartsick. I put some feed out for Leather, then tore off a chunk of two-day-old bread for myself. Mama was likely saving it for a bread pudding, but I couldn't work on an empty stomach. The bread was so stale the crumbs made ticking noises as they hit the wood floor. And here I was trying to wash it down with coffee that tasted like vinegar.

Papa laid the egg basket on the table. "Your mama ain't feeling well this morning. The heat's gotten to her."

The heat of your words, I thought.

"You'll have to gather the eggs and milk the cows this morning. Or you can pitch hay while I milk. Don't make no mind to me. The supplies I bought yesterday are still on the wagon, so we'll take 'em out near sunup and rebuild the fence."

Papa talked in a low tone, but his commands still came across normal. He looked like he'd already put in a full day, but then, the way I felt, I probably did, too. I saw the strongbox sitting on the kitchen counter, wide open. Why had Ethan taken the money? Had he taken it all at once, or snuck a little at a time? It wasn't his nature to steal. But then I remembered hearing Buster and Dale saying that Ethan still owed them money.

Papa pushed open the back door, waking me from my pondering. Grabbing the egg basket, I hurried out.

The chicken coop smelled, and I knew that cleaning it was one more chore I'd be stuck with. Some of the eggs had rolled out of their nests into the chicken mess. I had to be careful picking them up in the dark. It felt odd being out here so early, while the hens were still asleep. I don't think Mama gathered eggs this time of the morning, but Papa was probably trying to get things scheduled out so he and I could fit all the work into one day.

The sun was coming up as we headed out to the pasture in the wagon. Leather had hitched a ride in the back, his ears and tongue bouncing as we rolled along. The morning hadn't broke enough to shed good light, and the dead cornstalks looked more pitiful in the dawn. Brown and brittle, like ancient skeletons clambered together in a heap. I didn't bother looking at the cotton field. I knew it would look worse.

The men had been through here again. The watering tank had been trampled, and fresh hoofprints marked the ground. Papa didn't say a word, just unloaded the wagon like it was an everyday task. I didn't wait for his instructions. I grabbed the hammer and nails and helped him slide some of the barbed wire out. My mouth was already feeling puckered, both from the heat and Papa's buzzard-flavored coffee. I didn't dare get a drink of water this early. I had to show Papa how tough I was. Leather was smart, though. He was already at the watering tank, lapping up large mouthfuls.

We hammered, strung, and nailed for a while. Papa patched a much better fence than Ethan. And with less effort. He didn't bother about rattlesnakes or daydreaming. He set to work and got it done. I fumbled the nails a few times and slipped once while holding a fence post. Papa didn't even gripe, even though I could see the impatience on his face.

It took the better part of the morning to mend the fence. We reached down and splashed our faces with water. Leather thought it was a game and ran in, wagging his tail and whimpering to play. When we got back into the wagon Papa sat there, looking at the fence. I don't think he was really seeing it though. Finally he said, "Be good to your mama, son."

"Yes, sir." I wondered why he'd say that. I was always good to Mama.

"Don't never break her heart. You understand that?"

I could see the hurt in Papa's eyes, but I don't think he was hurting for Ethan 'cause Papa could hold a grudge till the end of time. He was hurting for Mama. He'd taken Ethan away from her. I guess he was expecting me to fill my brother's shoes. But that's a task too big for me.

CHAPTER SEVEN

THERE ARE FOUR KINDS OF sleep—restless, light, peaceful, and dead to the world. Dead to the world was how I slept. I fell into bed before the sun set, and woke up long after it had reached the treetops. Every part of my body ached, especially my arms. Doing mine and Ethan's chores is one thing, but doing Mama's work, and mending fences to boot, that's more than a fellow can stand.

I woke up smelling bacon, and my stomach gave a deep low growl. I hurried into the kitchen to find my plate sitting on the table. It'd been there a while. The eggs had an orange tinge to them, and the grits were just one hard lump. I didn't care. I dug into it like it was my last meal. I could taste that it wasn't Mama's cooking, but it'd do.

Papa came in carrying a bowl of peas to shell. He set it down on the table.

"Where's Mama?" I asked.

Papa pulled a handkerchief from his pocket and wiped his forehead. "Your mama is in repose."

"Uh—what?" I nearly choked on my scrambled eggs. I knew what *in repose* meant, but I'd never heard Papa use any two-dollar words like that before.

"She's resting," he said, sounding angry.

Resting? Grieving was more like it. I'd about gobbled down my whole breakfast when I remembered what day it was. I hurried to Mama's bedroom and quietly knocked as I opened the door. "Mama?"

She was lying in bed, staring out the window with empty eyes. Her hair stuck out like broom straw. At first I thought she was dead, but I saw her chest moving softly up and down, and a moment later she blinked.

"Mama, it's Sunday. What about church?"

Mama never missed church. And she never accepted any excuses from me and Ethan for missing, either.

"Mama?" I walked over and sat down on the end of her bed. A morning breeze had kicked up and was causing the lace curtain to puff out like a sail.

She turned her head and looked at me. I barely recognized her. Her face was a mask of hopelessness. "I'm not going to church today," she said. "I don't have the strength."

"Can I get you something? Some coffee or tea? Maybe you should eat."

She reached for me, and I took her hand. "I just want to rest."

I pushed the curtains aside so she could get the fuller extent of the breeze. Leaving her room, my heart felt as heavy as an ox.

When I got back to the kitchen Papa was sharpening a knife on a whetstone. "Get the water boiling under the wash pots outside."

"I gotta wash clothes?"

He looked up at me, his face pinched. "Saturday wash didn't get done."

"But God says people ain't supposed to work on Sunday. It's holy."

"So is my socks, but you're gonna wash 'em today, no matter what God says." He blew the shavings off the knife and went out the back door. I knew better than to stay inside.

The heat of the fire hitting those black wash pots just added to the blazes already coming from the sun. It was merciless. I wanted to be in the shade, but the fire had to be contained. It couldn't be too close to trees or bushes, especially as dry as the ones on our property. Rolling up my sleeves, I grabbed the washboard and went about scrubbing. What a god-awful job! No wonder Mama's knuckles were always calloused and red. I scraped mine constantly until I got the hang of it. Washing in one pot, rinsing in another. I'd scrubbed most of the clothes when I heard a buckboard pulling up to the side of the house.

Mary Ann stepped off, all dressed in her Sunday church clothes. Her hair was golden ringlets, and her eyes as bright as the sun itself. She smiled at me. I smiled back until I realized

I was standing there like a fool, holding Papa's drawers in my hands. I quickly dropped them in the wash pot and wiped the soap off on my trousers.

"I know I should have gone to the front door," she said, "but I saw the smoke coming from back here and thought maybe y'all were having a cookout."

I remembered then that Mama had invited her for Sunday dinner. "Mary Ann, I—"

"Y'all weren't at church this morning," she said, cutting me off.

Usually I would have thought that was rude, but I remembered that she was who she was—one of those girls who loved to wag her tongue. Ethan used to say she gave him an earache some nights, and he'd leave her house and go to the saloon for some peace and quiet.

"We weren't at church. See, Mama's not feeling well, and—"

"Oh dear! Is she bad off?" She didn't wait for an answer, but headed for the back door. I rushed in after her.

She looked at the dirty kitchen with eggs drying on breakfast plates. "I'll get that," I said to her. I picked up the plates and set them on the back porch for Leather. He could clean them faster than any dishwasher in the county. Mary Ann gave me a look like I was some bum who'd just rode into town.

She whipped around to the hallway, clutching her fancy little fringy bag in her hands, and peeped into Mama's bedroom. I would have thought that was rude, too, but she was who she was.

Mama was asleep, her soft snores keeping time with the

ticking clock. Mary Ann closed the door as softly as she'd opened it. "Is she running a fever?"

"No."

"Are you sure?"

"Well …"

"There's something going around."

"Yes, but … "

She squinted at me. "Did you call a doctor?"

"No."

"Why not?"

"Because she's not really—"

"You should call a doctor, Jesse. A fever is dangerous."

"She doesn't have a—"

"Well, I came here for dinner, but it looks like there ain't nothing to eat."

I waited. No point in me trying to get a word in.

"Except … that big apple pie I brought with me." She grinned and rustled her skirt as she swept by me. "I'll just go get it out of the buggy."

Papa stormed in about then, not paying attention. "What the hell is wrong with you, boy? You trying to make garment soup?" He stopped abruptly when he saw Mary Ann, then removed his hat. "I'm sorry. Didn't know we had company."

"Mary Ann brought us an apple pie." I was hoping she planned to leave it with us and head off.

"I could sure go for some apple pie," Papa said, forcing a polite smile.

Mary Ann lowered her head, kind of bashful. "I'll be right back."

No sooner was she out the door when Papa grabbed me by the collar. "Get out there and mind those clothes," he whispered. "You can finish washing them later."

Apple pie and buttermilk. I can't think of a better Sunday dinner. Papa and I had two big slices each. Mary Ann just toyed with hers, her pinky sticking out. I can't imagine rearranging a slice of pie instead of eating it, but then I figured she was probably wearing one of those corsets that barely made enough room for breathing.

"Fence-cutters destroyed my Uncle Herbert's fence last night."

Papa laid down his fork. "Is that the first time?"

"I think so," Mary Ann said. "Aunt Ethel said they cut about a half a mile of it, but she does exaggerate."

"Maybe not," Papa said. "Those men are capable. We need some laws passed, and we need 'em fast."

"Aunt Ethel says that they're thinking of going to Austin to talk to Governor Ireland. They'll camp out on his doorstep until they've been heard."

I was thinking Mary Ann should go with them. Let her start talking and the governor would pass a law quick, just to get rid of her.

"That's a sound idea," Papa said, talking about the trip to Austin. "You tell Herbert if he needs any help mending that fence, that Jesse and I would be glad to lend a hand."

I nearly dropped my fork. Like we don't have enough to do around here! And I sure haven't seen Herbert Cummings and his fat wife, Ethel, over here mending our fence.

Mary Ann kept talking, but I mostly shut her out. I did notice that she looked around as she spoke—out the window, out the back door, even craning her neck to see down the hall toward Ethan's bedroom. I know what she was itching to ask, but I prayed she didn't in front of Papa. When Papa got up to take some pie and buttermilk in to Mama, I thought Mary Ann would explode. "Where's your brother? Shouldn't he be here, helping to tend your mama?"

"Shhh …" I put my finger over my lips. "I'll tell you when you're ready to leave. We can't talk about it out loud."

I wanted to kill two birds with one stone. I'd be able to tell her about Ethan without Papa hearing, but mostly I was hoping she'd be so anxious to hear that she'd excuse herself right then. She only nodded at me and took a sip of buttermilk.

"Your mother has always been so kind to us and the folks at church. If only I were as good a Christian as her. I feel I need to do something to repay her. I'm going to stay a while, Jesse, and help you with this kitchen. Where does your mama keep her apron?"

Why did Mama have to be such a good Christian? "In the pantry, hanging on a nail."

"Well," she said, tying it on. "Let's start shelling these peas."

I looked out back at the piled-up washing that needed to be hung on the clothesline. Suddenly, it seemed like the happiest chore in the world.

I got a potent earful of everything about everybody before Mary Ann decided to leave. She even gossiped about folk I didn't know! I swear to Pete, I wish we could plow as fast as she could run her mouth. But when we finally walked out to her buckboard, I knew she wouldn't leave until I told her about Ethan. It was the first time all day she was dumbstruck. She held her face tight like someone holding back a good cry, and I didn't know what to think other than maybe I should have kept my mouth shut, too.

CHAPTER EIGHT

THE NEXT MORNING WE WERE OFF to the back pasture again, and a discovery that turned our blood to ice. I swear to Pete, if I lived to be a hundred years old, and visited every slaughterhouse in every corner of the world, I'd never again see anything so horrible. Someone had played wrangler with our newborn calf, but instead of rope, he used the long strands of our barbed-wire fence. She was sliced up like a holiday ham. Lots worse than the necklace they'd made for Old Leather Dog.

"Jesse! Hold her legs still!" Papa yelled.

I wanted to help Papa, but the more barb I tried to unwind, the more tangled she got. Blood gushed from her like water from a rusted-out bucket.

Leather Dog pounced and circled, growling like he'd treed a coon.

"Shut that bald hound dog up!" Papa shouted as he sliced the palm of his glove on a barb.

"Leather, come here, boy." Leather circled wide around the calf and settled next to me. "Now, hush up," I said, trying to sit on the calf's hooves to keep her still.

Papa worked and worked, but it seemed like that calf had a mile of barbed wire dug into her flesh. I couldn't look away without my eyes straying to the threatening note that had also been left behind.

"How could anyone do a thing like this?" I asked, speaking of the threat as well as the calf.

Papa snorted. "They're devils," he said, "fence-cutting devils. The good Lord help 'em if I find out who they are."

I watched the calf struggle, but her movements began to slow. Her eyes glazed over like frosted glass windows as her spirit drained like the blood from her hide.

Papa sat back on his haunches and wiped the sweat from his forehead, leaving a dark crimson streak above his eyebrows. The sun was barely up, but the heat already burned a haze across the pasture.

Papa stopped pulling barbed wire and looked over at me. He shook his head. I thought we were just gonna sit there and watch that calf die, but then he said, "Grab the shotgun, son."

I just stood there, still as one of the fence posts.

"Get the shotgun. Put this thing out of her misery." He gave me a nod like it was the most natural thing in the world. "Go on."

I shuffled over to Papa's horse, not really in any hurry to witness him putting her out of her misery. My shirt was sticking to me, partly from sweat, partly from calf's blood.

I handed the gun toward Papa, who was leaning on a

fence post and tapping his hat on his pant leg. He slicked back his hair and put his hat back on. "Go ahead, shoot her," he said calmly.

"Me?"

"Yes, you!" I could feel the sting in his voice.

I couldn't believe he was putting this off on me. Was this a test? Would shooting this calf prove to him that I wasn't just a mama's boy without the gumption to do a man's job? I hadn't aimed a gun since the day Smokey died. And this one suddenly felt as heavy as a sack of horse shoes.

Sweat poured faster, and it wasn't from the heat. But I knew better than to open my mouth again. Papa stood, watching. I brought the butt of the shotgun up and rested it on my shoulder. Cradling it softly, I stared down the barrel at the squirming calf. She wallowed in a bed of sticky mud that looked a lot like the dewberry preserves that Mama canned every spring. I placed my finger on the trigger.

"Well, what are you waiting for?" Papa asked.

I just kept looking down that barrel. The sun burned into my back and sweat dripped into my eye. I took my finger off the trigger to flick the sweat away.

"Come on!" Papa yelled.

I gripped the gun tightly, like it weighed a ton. I could barely hold it still. And seeing Papa from the corner of my eye, he was starting to squirm, too. "Get on with it!" he hollered.

I took a deep breath and aimed again. Getting my finger to squeeze that trigger was like getting a mule to pull a locomotive. It wouldn't budge.

Papa came over and yanked the shotgun from my hands,

shoving me aside. "Never mind!" he snarled. Before I could say a word, he flipped the gun up to his shoulder and pulled the trigger. The blast echoed through the distance, leaving a ringing in my ear. Leather buried his head under his paws and whined. I was wishing I could do the same.

The calf lay as still as a rock, now with blood oozing between her eyes. It made me think of Smokey lying on the ground, his eyes rolled up white, blood gushing from the wound. Why'd he jump at the wrong moment? Why'd the bird I was targeting take flight right then? Why was I such a sorry aim? I could ask why over and over, but it wouldn't retract what happened to Smokey ... or me.

"It was a mercy killin'," Papa said, talking about the calf.

I couldn't argue. Barbed wire sprang out of her here and there like a metal cactus—unfair treatment for an animal that had only been in this world a couple of weeks. I was doing everything in my power to keep my breakfast in my stomach. It threatened to come up again and again, a couple of times making it all the way to my throat. I choked it back down so Papa wouldn't have something else to humiliate me about.

He turned and faced me. "I'll drag her carcass to the barn for now to get rid of these buzzards. You get the hammer and nails."

I jolted. "We're not going to fix the fence again, are we?"

"Who else is going to do it?" Papa said, shaking his head.

"How many times are we going to just keep rebuilding it? How many?"

Papa stared at me, his eyes dark.

"Besides," I continued, "it's dangerous!"

"Not as dangerous as a boy questioning the decisions of his father. You'll do as I say, or you'll feel the end of the strap. Don't make no nevermind to me."

I felt as bound up as that calf, and his words dug into me like the pointed barbs. I had no choice.

Papa dusted his hat on his leg again, then walked over to the calf. I picked up the shotgun, his ripped gloves, and the note that had been tacked to the crosswire. Someone had carefully scrawled the words to disguise their own handwriting. I looked at the message again.

Next time this will be you!

CHAPTER NINE

THE SUN SCORCHED US PRETTY GOOD as Papa and I restrung the fence. Old Leather Dog stayed under the shade tree. He didn't want his bare hide burning, and heck, his skin looked leathery enough without the sun tanning it. I kept praying for a cool breeze. Just one. That would have been as refreshing as a drink of water. But the morning was still and quiet except for a few dryflies crying for rain.

Papa concentrated on the fence, not saying a word. Did he have a plan for the fence-cutters? If he did, he wasn't fessin' up. And I figured he was still mad that I didn't pull the trigger. It was no use trying to explain why. He knew well enough. To Papa I was yellow as a bee, with no sting at all.

Within the quiet, my mind wondered about Ethan. *Where did he go? What's he doing?*

Once we had that fence mended, Papa stood up tall and stretched. I heard the bones cracking in his back. I tried it, too, but only managed to irritate the sunburn on my neck. I studied that shiny new portion of the fence, then looked at Papa. "This is suicide. They'll just come back again tonight. Cut it down ... or worse."

"That ain't nothing for you to worry about," he said, gathering up the tools. "Let's go see if we still have some of that buttermilk left."

He turned his back to me and headed over to the wagon. I followed behind with Leather tailing us both. Not worry? How could Papa ignore that note? I just didn't understand. In the past the fence-cutters only snuck around cutting fences. Now they were torturing innocent animals and leaving threats. I looked down at the scars on Leather's neck. Worried? Yep, I was worried.

As we neared the house I saw someone walking toward us carrying a scythe and hoe over one shoulder. They both towered above him, but he strode along, balancing them with no problem at all. I couldn't mistake that gait. It was Pud Taylor.

"I come to clean out that cornfield, Mister Wade." He pronounced it Misser.

Papa nodded. "And we need to see what we can salvage of the cotton field, too."

Pud nodded back.

"I didn't think we had any money to pay extra help," I said, taking off my hat and scratching my head like the town fool. "We sure don't have enough crops to share."

Pud grinned a mile and a half. "Mister Wade promised to give me— "

"You ain't getting nothing if you don't get busy," Papa cut in. "Now git on with you."

"Yes, sir." Pud hurried past us.

"What'd you promise Pud?" I asked Papa as we took the horses to the barn.

"None of your concern," he answered, not looking my way. "Just be glad I didn't set you to doing field work. Unless you want to join him."

I knew when to keep my mouth shut.

The sun was a yellow bubble in the west, slanting toward us as Papa and I took the wagon into town for more supplies. I could barely see Main Street through all the dust the horses kicked up. A few folks milled about on foot. We stopped for two ladies crossing the street, fluttering paper fans to cool off.

As we carried on, we passed the saloon. My heart ached when I saw it. Had Ethan been there last night? A pale woman stood inside, peering out above the swinging doors. She looked like a prisoner staring out of a jail cell. Her face was ashen, and her eyes hollow. She appeared to be about Mama's age, and just as lifeless as Mama the last couple of days. The woman offered a weary smile, and wiggled her fingers at me in a slight wave. I nodded a little, not wanting Papa to see me being familiar with someone in a saloon. It wasn't until we'd gone past that I realized who the woman was. Mabel. I hadn't recognized her without all the face paint and the beauty mark. And the other night, I would have never guessed her age.

We stopped in front of the blacksmith shop, where Mr.

Isley pounded on his anvil. It was hard enough to breathe in this July heat, but stepping into that shop sucked all the air right out of my lungs. Satan himself would have been at home there.

"What can I do for you gentlemen?" Mr. Isley asked, smiling through a few black teeth.

"Nails," Papa said. "Big ones." He stretched out his fingers to show how long.

Mr. Isley dug through a wooden bin and brought out a handful of long nails. I got the feeling he was itching to say something as he slowly dropped them into a sack. He finally got the nerve.

"How'd you fare last night?" he asked, looking away.

"I didn't fare well at all," Papa said. "They cut my fence to bits."

Papa didn't mention the calf or the note. Guess he had too much weighing on his mind to get into that discussion.

I glanced up and noticed a large pair of wire cutters hanging on the wall. They looked harmless, really. Not as threatening as a gun. But I guess the real power of a tool is in how it's used.

"I hope they catch those scoundrels soon," Mr. Isley said, sounding a tad more sincere. "H. L. Blanton was hit hard. They cut over a mile of fence on his ranch."

"That's a shame," Papa said. "What we need is justice … or rain. Either one will stop them. Although right now justice sounds like a better deal."

"By the way," Mr. Isley said cautiously, not meeting Papa's eyes, "I saw your boy Ethan in here on Saturday."

My heart raced as I searched Papa's face, but he kept a stern, hard look. "I don't have a boy named Ethan."

"Come on, Tom," Mr. Isley said. "He's just a boy, and besides—"

"How much do I owe you?" Papa said, cutting him off.

I mustered up enough guts to speak. "Was he looking for a job?"

"Shush up, Jesse!" Papa warned.

Mr. Isley ignored Papa and gave me a gentle look. "I reshoed his horse. He was heading out of town."

My heart sank into my gullet. Papa paid for the nails.

"Anything else?" Mr. Isley asked.

Papa raised an eyebrow. "Yeah. I also need you to make me a couple of bear traps."

"Bear traps?" Mr. Isley asked, gazing at Papa thoughtfully.

"Yep. With very sharp teeth," Papa added.

Papa's spirits had lifted a little by the time we crossed the street, heading to the dry goods store. He even wore a crooked smile. Was he *that* happy Ethan had gone for good, or did he know something that the rest of the world hadn't caught on to?

As we walked by Mr. Tucker's barber pole, Roy Davis, a neighboring rancher, poked his head out of the barbershop door and smiled. "Tom, step in a minute."

The smell of pipe tobacco and warm menthol hung heavy in the air. The barbershop was the one place in town where the men did their congregating. Two men sat, thumbing through the newspaper, and two more were involved in a game of checkers.

Mr. Tucker sat in his own barber chair with his bulky legs crossed. He snapped his straight razor open and shut in a cold bracing rhythm. "Looks like you need a haircut, boy." His low gaze was settled on me. I took off my hat, ran my hands through my hair, and pushed my hat back on, figuring that was answer enough. No one else even looked up.

Roy Davis motioned Papa over where he and another rancher, Butch Peterson, stood talking to a tall, wiry stranger. I wasn't too happy about who they'd befriended. I recognized him right away—the stranger who'd sat at the bar the other night in the saloon. He was smiling and conversing, and with the daylight reflecting in his eyes, he didn't look near as sinister as he did then. Mr. Peterson, still grinning, said, "This here's the man you need to talk to." He reached over and slapped Papa on the back. "Meet Tom Wade and his boy, Jesse."

The stranger extended his hand. "Howdy. I'm Jackson Slater."

He shook Papa's hand, then mine. "Pleasure," I said, hoping he wouldn't say a word about seeing me before.

"Jackson rode in a few days ago, Tom," Mr. Davis explained. "He's looking for work."

"So which one of you is going to hire him?" Papa asked.

Both men laughed. "Butch and I have plenty of help. But I was telling Jackson how short-handed you are since that no-good son of yours is gone. You can't do it alone."

No doubt that meddling Mary Ann had her day in town, gossiping about Ethan with that pointed tongue of hers. My blood started to boil. These men had no right to judge Ethan. And then to think Papa was doing all the work alone. I was doing my chores and most of Ethan's. And lately, Mama's too. But they'd always ignored me anyway, so why should they think I exist now?

"I manage," Papa said. "Nice meeting you, Mr. Slater." He turned and walked out. I followed. It was just a few paces to the dry goods store, and Papa's stride urged me to catch up with him.

Mr. Slater stepped in behind me.

"I work cheap," he said, moving up next to Papa.

"You'd have to," Papa said. "My money's done disappeared."

"I work hard."

Papa turned to me and grinned. "Jesse, there ain't nothing worse than hearing a man beg."

I kinda got the feeling Papa liked Mr. Slater right off, though I don't rightly know why.

Mr. Slater kept on. "I can mend fences faster than a snake can swallow a chicken egg."

"Can you handle a gun?" Papa asked.

"If you loan me one." He looked a bit defeated.

Papa picked up some spices and laid a few coins on the counter. Then he grabbed a couple of peppermint sticks and tossed another penny in the pile. He handed me the candy as we walked toward the door.

"No gun," Papa said, shaking his head.

"If you loan me a gun," Mr. Slater continued, "I can shoot a wild hair off a hound dog."

Papa and I looked at each other and laughed out loud.

"That would be impossible at our house," Papa said. "But come on anyway. I'll find something useful for you to do."

I couldn't believe what just happened. We had no money, but he had Pud clearing the dead crops, and now he was hiring a work hand? Made no sense to me. But Papa seemed in decent spirits, so I left well enough alone.

The ride home was extra bumpy for me. Papa and Mr. Slater rode up on the seat while I lay back in the wagon bed, sucking on a peppermint. As we passed along the open road, the sky was all I could see. And I imagined myself falling, plunging straight down from the heavens. I loved the feel of it. It was only when we'd hit a rut in the road that I would snap out of my fall and back to reality.

When we got home Papa showed Mr. Slater the one-room shack behind the barn. Mr. Slater flung his saddlebag on the cot and patted the potbelly stove. Then he turned and looked out the side window. "And the outhouse is right over there," he said, grinning. "This'll do."

"We'll see that you get dinner," Papa said. "Jesse will bring it out later."

"Much obliged." Mr. Slater smiled at us like Papa had set him up in a palace.

Papa hurried to the house, but I hung back some. I didn't know what to make of Jackson Slater. He looked rugged enough to be a hired hand with his bushy black hair and thick mustache, but his fine horse and clean clothes didn't match up to a man who would beg for a job. Some days are just full of things to ponder, but I was too tuckered to do any pondering right then.

CHAPTER TEN

MR. SLATER LOOKED MIGHTY HUNGRY when I handed him a heaping plate of food. He sat on the cot and dug right in—not an easy thing to do with Papa's cooking.

"You eat yet?" he asked through a mouthful of mashed potatoes.

"Yep," I said, still standing in the doorway.

"Why don't you come in, keep me company?" He kicked a rickety wooden chair, sliding it toward me. I sat down.

"Where are you from, Mr. Slater?"

"Call me Jackson."

"Papa might think that's disrespectful."

"What's disrespectful about talking down to the hired help?" he asked, stabbing the string beans with his fork.

Old Leather Dog appeared in the doorway. He was trained well enough to know better than to enter a house—even one as shabby as this.

"What in tarnation is that?" Jackson asked as Leather knelt down and laid his head on his paws.

"That's my dog."

"Why he's as slick as a sliver!" Jackson looked like he didn't know whether to be shocked or to bust out laughing.

"When I found him a couple of years ago, he had a severe case of the mange. I bathed him every day in creosote, and doctored his sores with salve. He got better, but his hair never did grow back. Papa took to calling him Old Leather Dog. I just call him Leather." I didn't mention that saving Old Leather Dog was one of my ways of making up for what happened to Smokey. That wasn't nobody's business but mine. And while Leather didn't turn out to be a cow dog, he did turn out to be the best friend I've ever had.

Jackson laid his fork down for a moment and wiped his upper lip. "You couldn't have picked a better name for him," he said, shaking his head. "Those welts on his neck look bad. Those bee stings?"

"He got stung all right." His wounds from the barbed wire were still swollen and pink.

Jackson went back to eating, and I sat, waiting for him to finish so I could take his plate back to the house. Save myself a trip later when I washed dishes. My eyes darted to everything in the shack, trying not to stare at Jackson. After a few more swallows of food, he looked up again.

"So that was your brother you were with in the saloon the other night, right?"

I nodded, wondering if he could see the fire in my cheeks. "You ain't gonna tell Papa about that, are you?"

Jackson sniffed like he was considering what I said. "Your personal business is yours, I guess. But you must miss him."

"I miss him sometimes," I said, not wanting to reveal too much. Heck, Ethan had only been gone for two days, but I did miss him a lot.

"Where do you think he went?"

That seemed like an awful nosy question from someone who'd just said my personal business was mine. "Someplace better than this," I answered.

"Better than what?" Jackson asked. "Home or Texas?"

"Both," I said. "Figure he got tired of mending fences."

Jackson laughed. "If he's in Texas, that's probably all he's doing."

We were quiet for a moment, then Jackson spoke again. "You think he got very far with your papa's money?"

I felt the anger churning inside me like a tornado sweeping through the fields. I don't know if he heard that from Papa or the men in town, but it didn't set right with me. "He don't have Papa's money! He used it to pay off gambling debts. He made a mistake, that's all. Why can't people understand that? Why can't people forgive?"

"Whoa ... slow down, son," Jackson said, settling the plate on his knee. "I'm not the person to yell at." He sniffed again and brushed his mustache with his fingers. "Who knows? Maybe your papa will come around eventually. See the light."

I took a deep breath to settle myself. "You sure don't know my papa. And besides, right now he's only concerned with the fence-cutters. I heard him say that he's gonna send a letter to the governor, asking him to do something about them.

It doesn't make sense. How can a man think it's all right to destroy another man's fence?"

"You've got to understand," Jackson said. "Texas was wide open country. Men were used to driving their cattle anywhere there was water. They don't like being fenced out."

"But it's our property!"

He raised an eyebrow. "I know a whole lot of Indians that would argue with you about that."

"So, whose side are you on anyway?" I asked, getting mad all over again.

"Let's just say I try to keep an open mind."

I snatched the empty plate from him. "You might want to keep that kind of thinking to yourself," I said before stomping out the door. Leather trotted at my heels as I ran back to the house. Walking in, I realized something. Jackson asked me a lot of questions, but he never once answered mine.

I put the dishes in the kitchen, then snuck into Ethan's old room. I took comfort being in there. But some shuffling from the closet made me freeze in my tracks. I craned my neck to see who was there. Out came Pud, holding a couple of Ethan's shirts and a pair of britches.

"You little thief! What the heck do you think you're doing?"

Pud's grin was a mile wide. "Getting paid," he said. "Mr. Wade promised to give me some of Ethan's clothes if I cleared the crops."

"He can't do that."

I didn't think it was possible, but Pud grinned even bigger. "He did."

"You know it ain't right."

Pud stuffed the clothes in an old burlap bag. "Ain't right? What ain't right is cinching your belt when you ain't et nothing for two days. What ain't right is using your worn out clothes to cut patches for your other worn out clothes. Don't preach to me, Jesse Wade. I earned these clothes, and I'm taking 'em."

Pud was right. I didn't have any reason to be mad at him. It was Papa who was causing everything to be cattywampus around here. "Well, get what's yours and get out," I said.

Pud knelt down, running his fingers over Ethan's fancy alligator boots. "I sure would like to take these."

"You didn't work that hard," I said, trying to control the heat in my voice. Ethan would have ninety-nine fits if someone got away with this prize boots.

Pud dragged the burlap sack behind him as he left. He'd only taken a few things. After all, he wasn't fool-headed. He had to leave something behind for Papa to pay him with again. Or had Papa promised some to Jackson?

After he'd gone, I sat in the back corner for a while. Every inch of this room was Ethan. Would this be the closest I'd ever get to him again? I looked out the window at the shack out back. I could see a lantern glowing, but that was it. Jackson Slater. What was he doing in there anyway? I needed a closer look.

I slipped out to the barn and climbed up to the hayloft, opening the wood shutter just enough to let a sliver of moonlight fall on the hay. I now had a better view of the shack, but there wasn't much to see. The lantern still glowed through the window, and occasionally I'd see Jackson's shadow cross behind the flour sack curtains. I laid my head on my arms and kept watching. I don't know when Jackson put out his light. The mellow scent of the hay lulled me into a deep sleep.

The next light I saw was the pink sun pushing up into the sky.

"Jesse! Where the heck are you?" It was Papa, and he sounded angry. I wasn't sure whether to run, hide, or fess up.

"Up here, Papa," I called down, quickly knocking the hay from my hair and collar.

"What in the hell are you doing sleeping up there?"

I looked down and saw Papa with his hands hanging at his sides. At least he wasn't holding the strap. Jackson stood behind him with a worried look.

I stuttered and mumbled. Getting caught had made my mind a sieve. He'd probably wallop me anyway.

"Never mind!" Papa yelled as I climbed down the ladder, still trying to think of what to say. "Come on! We've got trouble."

We sure did. We rode out to the back where our fence had once again been shredded and chopped into bits. The thorny barbed pieces were scattered like leaves. But that wasn't the worst. Two of our cows lay dead on the ground, their throats slit.

The heat and the smell had already brought the flies. They swarmed and fed and droned in the sticky mess. My stomach did the usual lurch, and I was mighty thankful I'd missed breakfast.

Jackson dismounted from his horse and wandered over

to a fence post. He ripped off another note, glanced at it, then handed it to Papa. Papa nodded.

"Jackson, I think it's time I loaned you a gun," he said, pitching the note down on the ground. From where I sat, I could just make out the words.

This is your final warning!

CHAPTER ELEVEN

JACKSON PROVED TO BE A big help that day. Sweat
didn't bother him. I didn't hang around, though. I spent my
time on other chores, avoiding Papa and Jackson both. And I
hadn't thought up one decent excuse yet to tell Papa why I was
sleeping in the barn.

Jackson didn't rebuild the fence that day, and I was
thankful. Stringing up a new fence would be like stringing
up a noose. No sense in hanging ourselves. The fence-cutters
proved to us more than once to be brutal and heartless, and
that note wasn't just a scrap of worthless paper. Those five
words held our future—a future that was looking more dark
and dangerous each night.

Mama was up and about again even though she looked

like the walking dead. Could losing your son really rip your soul clean away?

As the day rolled on, I helped her out. We gathered the afternoon eggs in the chicken coop while the hens pecked at their feed. I watched Mama grab two eggs at a time and place them in the basket. Worry lines creased her forehead. Her blue eyes, usually soft as corn silk, looked dark and stormy. I wanted to make things right for her, to ease her mind, but I could never take Ethan's place. He had always been her strength. He drove her to church every Sunday, sitting high on the wagon, Mama right next to him with her parasol shading her pale face. He had always made her proud. And now she only had me—a poor substitute. But I had to try. Ethan may have stole Papa's money, but heck, did he have to take Mama's spirit, too?

I figured this fence-cutting business was also weighing heavy in her thoughts. I decided to speak up, thinking she might need someone to talk to.

"Did you meet Jackson?" I asked.

"Briefly," she said. That was all.

"Well, what do you think of him?"

"He seems like a nice man. Very polite. Rather handsome, too. But we need the extra help, and that's all that matters."

That's not all that matters! I wanted to scream. *Everything matters! Ethan. The fences. The drought. Everything!* How could she be so calm? Was I the only one feeling our lives were on a short fuse?

Mama kept gathering eggs like I wasn't even there. I couldn't take it anymore. We'd all been pulled apart since that night. I wanted to say something. I had to. "Mama, I miss Ethan."

Mama froze in her spot, tears welling in her eyes. "Hush, Jesse!" she whispered. "You know we're not allowed to say his name."

"But Papa ain't here. He can't hear us."

Mama turned to me, her face ghost white. "We can't talk about him anymore. He's dead."

"But he's not dead, Mama. He's alive. I miss him and I know you do, too. Look at you. Look at what Papa's done. Ethan made a mistake. Why can't he see that?"

"Oh Jesse," Mama said. "I miss him, too. He's on my mind every minute of the day. I lost my son … my son." Tears welled in her eyes. She gathered up a corner of her apron and dabbed at them. Then she looked out onto the pasture, like she was seeing beyond it. "I'd never seen Ethan raise his hand to Papa before …"

It was self-defense, I wanted to say. But stating that wouldn't help her. It might send her back to bed with the vapors. And I'd have failed her, too.

Mama continued to stare out of the chicken coop, probably wondering if she could have done something different. Something to smooth things over. I walked up next to her and placed my hand on her shoulder. "It's okay, Mama. You and I can talk about Ethan, secretly. We know he didn't mean to hurt no one."

She turned toward me, her eyes as big as an owl's. "What's wrong with you, Jesse? He took everything but my grandmother's silver tea service. We're left with no savings. And you know we have to respect your father's wishes. You're thirteen now. Try to act like a man."

I just stood there, dumbfounded. Had she done a complete turnaround? Was she siding with Papa?

You can't forgive him either? I wondered.

Mama brushed my hand off her shoulder and hurried out of the coop, her dress sweeping the ground. I heard a few muffled sobs escape her as she went. I followed behind her, not daring to say another word.

CHAPTER TWELVE

WHEN WE GOT BACK TO THE HOUSE, Papa and
Jackson were standing by the gun cabinet.

"Here, take the rifle," Papa said, pulling it from the rack
and handing it over.

"That's Ethan's gun!" I blurted.

An awkward silence filled the room. "Try to act like a
man," Mama had said. Right now I wasn't sure how to act.
Papa stared hard at me like a wild bull ready to charge.

Jackson could sense the heat. His eyes darted from me to
Papa, and back to me.

Mama stood wringing her hands. The basket of eggs
rested on the crook of her elbow, bouncing against her hip. It's
a wonder none of those eggs cracked.

Jackson eyed the gun, then said to me, "Why can't I use
Ethan's rifle, Jesse?"

Now I was trapped like a rabbit in a snare. I shuffled my

feet, not sure what to say. But I was thinking, *'Cause Ethan will use it when he comes home.*

Papa's eyes glowed like brimstone, and I figured I was due for the strap for sure. Jackson must have figured that, too. I could tell he wanted to smooth things over. He smiled and winked and said, "Tell me, which one of these guns do you shoot?"

Not so smooth. I just stood there with my mouth hanging open while the fire sizzled hotter in Papa's eyes. "Jesse would rather get bit by a diamondback than shoot a gun," he said.

Jackson went back to studying the rifle. "There ain't nothing wrong with shooting in self-defense," he offered.

"Or to protect a man's property!" Papa added, a little calmer. "You take that gun, Jackson. I suspect we're gonna have more trouble than we can handle."

Jackson nodded. "Jesse, I'd be happy to teach you how to shoot," he said, resting the rifle in front of him. "Why don't we go out for a little target practice after supper?"

Warm bile rose into my throat. I wanted to say no, but didn't know how without looking like the coward I was.

"You're wasting your time," Papa said, closing the gun cabinet. "This boy never will grow up."

Mama's words echoed again. "Try to act like a man." She swept by, heading for the kitchen.

We rode out back late that afternoon with the sun resting just right in the sky, plenty of light, less heat. Jackson brought a burlap sack filled with old bottles. They clanked and chinked with a steady rhythm as we made our way to the fence. Lots of barbed-wire bits were still spread around from that last fence attack. Jackson kicked them aside with his boot as he walked to a post and propped a bottle.

"You ever shoot before?" he asked.

"Yeah. But not in a while." I figured that was all I had to say. Jackson didn't need to know the details, and I didn't want to tell him anyway. Wasn't nobody's business but mine.

"What kind of gun did you use?" he asked.

"Shotgun."

"Whew! Bet it knocked you on your behind."

I just nodded. Seemed Jackson figured I'd only shot a gun once in my whole life. I'd done lots of shooting … till about two years ago.

"Well, don't be afraid. This rifle doesn't have near as much kick." Jackson pulled it from his saddle holster and held it out with admiration. Most people think a gun should be respected more than just about anything else.

Jackson held it toward me, but I said, "You go first."

He chuckled. "And waste a bullet on that big old bottle just sitting still? Heck, at least let me nab a coon or a squirrel, something we can eat."

He aimed the rifle toward a tree, but I gently pushed the barrel aside. "No animals." I'd seen enough dead critters lately.

Jackson lowered the gun and looked at me with new understanding. "Okay, but I need a moving target. Chuck a bottle in the air as high as you can."

I stepped away to retrieve a bottle from the sack. When I lifted one out, Jackson said, "Uh-uh. Get that small one."

I know it was my idea for him to go first, but I couldn't

help but think he was just plain showing off. I grabbed the smallest one. "You ready?" I asked.

The rifle rested on Jackson's shoulder with the barrel pointing down. He gave a hard nod, and I pitched the bottle up and out, toward the fence post. In one swan-like swoop, he brought the gun up and shattered that bottle to smithereens. It showered down like giant crystals, glinting in the late sun.

"Pretty good," I said. Actually, it was great. He could probably shoot the sweat beads clean off my nose. Quite a skill for a man who didn't even *own* a gun.

Jackson smiled. "It's your turn."

My mouth went dry, so I grabbed the canteen and took a long drink. I knew I couldn't stall anymore, so I walked over to Jackson, took the gun, and faced the bottle.

"Plant your feet still," Jackson said.

I rested the butt of the rifle up near my chin.

"Don't choke up on the barrel, son. Relax."

I let out a deep breath, lowering my shoulders.

"That's it. That's it." Jackson's voice was as gentle as a lullaby.

I stared down the long, slim barrel. It seemed to stretch a mile.

"Both eyes open, Jesse." Jackson whispered now, like the noise might scare that bottle away.

I saw it, standing tall on that fence post.

"Gently squeeze the trigger."

I didn't. Odd thoughts ran through my head like wild Injuns.

Someone went through a lot of trouble to make that bottle. I didn't feel quite right blasting it away. I stared at it a little longer.

"You can do it," Jackson whispered, leaning forward.

My sweaty fingers stuck to the gun. I raised my trigger finger for just a moment, then placed it back. The bottle started to blur.

"Take your time. He's not moving." This time it wasn't Jackson's voice I heard. It was Ethan's. "Come on, Jesse, it's a quail. Shoot it."

I saw its feathers lying smooth against its breast. He chirruped and twittered, filling the air with his craggy tune.

"Shoot him before he flies away."

The shotgun was bigger then me, but I managed to hold it still. I loved Ethan more than anyone alive, and I couldn't disappoint him. I'd show him. I'd make him proud of his little brother. We'd be eating quail for dinner.

The echoes of that blast rang in my ears as I jerked backward, the gun bucking my shoulder.

The quail took flight, but Smokey, who'd snuck up on the bird as I shot, lay there still as a log.

"Holy Jehosaphat!" Ethan had cried, rushing to Smokey and kneeling by his lifeless body. "Jesse, what'd you do?"

He said it like that. Like I'd done it on purpose. I didn't answer him. I couldn't. My body was in shock. And it was nearly a week before I uttered a word. I got my voice back, but not my nerve. Not then. Not now.

I lowered the gun and handed it back to Jackson. The bottle still stood on that fence post in one piece, and that was just fine with me.

"Maybe another time," I said.

CHAPTER THIRTEEN

THE NEXT WEEK PASSED SLOW, everyone on edge. The fence-cutters hadn't stopped. Papa read in the newspaper about other ranchers in Texas having their fences whacked to bits, too. And the fence-cutters didn't just clip the wires, they were making bonfires with fence posts and setting pastures ablaze. Thousands of dollars in property had been destroyed. Papa banged his fist on the table. "It stops raining and folks just go crazy. What's the world coming to?"

I wish I knew myself. The cattle industry is big business, and like with any business a man's got to protect his investment. That's all Papa wanted to do, protect what was his.

Mama was a bit perkier, but still not speaking much. Her eyes were hollow, but there was an occasional spark.

I kept a keen eye on Jackson. I didn't trust him. He took to leaving at night and not coming back until after I'd gone to bed. I needed to know where he was riding off to, and what he did.

Jackson got friendly with Leather. Sometimes Leather

trotted behind him when he went to mend the back fence. But luckily, Jackson took his time about that. Papa told him not to string it all up at once. I'd snuck back there once or twice to see how he was getting on. He worked hard, but stopped every now and then to let out a powerful yawn. A sign that he was keeping some mighty late hours.

One evening after supper, when it was just too hot to stay in the house, Mama, Papa, and Leather and I sat out on the front porch. Leather jerked on an old piece of gnawed rope I held in my hand as we played tug-o-war. He bared his teeth and let out a low rolling playful growl. Jackson rode out, waving as he passed by.

"Where do you think he goes at night?" I asked Papa.

"I'm sure a handsome young man like Jackson has to go into town now and then to mingle some. He'd go plumb loco staying out here all the time."

"But he's gone *every* night," I said, rubbing the slick loose skin on Leather's neck.

"He's getting his work done, so where he goes at night ain't none of our business."

It's okay for Jackson, but not for Ethan.

Jackson never talked about his trips into town. He never mentioned folks he'd met or sat with at the saloon. He never brought back any news of what was going on with other ranchers or cowhands. Wouldn't a man who spent that much time in town at night have a powerful lot of friends by now? When Ethan spent his nights in town, he had an avalanche of gossip to share the next day—mostly about fights and ladies, and things he could never say in front of Mama. But some of it was news about the neighbors, their crops, and their cattle. But not Jackson. Where'd he really go each night? And what was he keeping from us?

Jackson hadn't been gone long when another rider came by. It was Butch Peterson, the rancher who'd introduced us to Jackson. He never got off his horse, just sat there big as you please and called up to Papa from the yard.

"Ho, Tom."

Papa stood up and stretched his suspenders. "What's wrong, Butch?"

Something had to be wrong. Mr. Peterson's farm was a good ten miles north of town. He wouldn't have come all this way just to chew the fat with Papa.

"Fence-cutters! That's what's wrong. Folks have had enough. Doesn't seem the governor's going to do anything about them, so it's left up to us. We're having a meeting at the church tomorrow night, eight o'clock. We need every rancher and farmer there."

"I'll be there," Papa assured him.

Mr. Peterson nodded. "Good. We're counting on you."

The next day Pud was back, helping Jackson mend the hen house. I wondered how many of Ethan's shirts he was earning today. Coyotes weren't near as good at ripping fences as the fence-cutters, but they tried awful hard. Luckily the only damage had been to the chicken wire, not the chickens. I'm guessing Leather did his job, chasing the coyotes away before they succeeded.

I carried some new salt licks out to the cows, and lazily took my time heading back. About noon, I went into the house for a bite to eat. I heard mumbling in the front room and peeked in. Mama was sitting on the couch next to Mary Ann. It looked like Mary Ann was doing most of the whispering, but Mama was nodding and staring, all caught up in whatever the big secret was. Some of what Mary Ann was saying drifted my way. Seemed like something about Ruth and Ethan. Did she know something we didn't?

When Mary Ann left, Mama came into the kitchen. "Mary Ann brought us a cherry pie and some fresh cream to pour over it. Would you like some?" She didn't wait for me to answer. She sliced off a gooey piece, and her hands trembled as she eased it into a bowl. That fresh cream splattered a little and rolled off the top. My mouth watered.

I pushed my plate of bread and cheese away like I never wanted to see it again. I'd barely dug the spoon into the pie when Mama sat down across from me. Her hands were fidgety, and her eyes looked anxious. Something big was up 'cause she never offered me dessert at lunchtime.

"You still got a lot to do today, Jesse?"

What kind of question was that? Mama knew the list, mostly consisting of me loading what bags of cotton we had to take to the cotton gin. "Some," I said through a mouthful of cherries.

Mama reached over and wiped some of the syrup from my chin. "I think those chores can wait a while." Then she dug into the pocket of her apron and brought out a folded piece of paper. When she opened it, I could tell it was some kind of hand-drawn map. She stared down at it for a moment, like it was a long lost letter. Something wasn't right. "I want you to take me here." She pointed to an X off one of the roads.

I took the map from her and looked it over. The road

led off from the south side of town. I hadn't been down there much. Mostly because there wasn't much down there. "Why are we going here?"

Mama stood up and removed her apron. "Just finish your pie and get the buggy."

She hurried about, her hands fluttering. I'd never seen her so agitated. And acting so secretive—like we'd be sneaking off or something. Wherever we were going would probably have Papa throwing a screaming fit. He might just disown us like he did Ethan. But curiosity ate at me so hard, I practically swallowed the rest of that pie in one giant gulp. I had the buggy ready to go before Mama got her big flowery hat pinned on straight.

I didn't drive her straight through town. I figured it was best to take some of the back roads out by the church, then circle around and hit Main Street just past the last shop. It took more than an hour, but lost time was better than greeting folks we didn't aim to see.

Mama swayed to the bumpy rhythm of the buggy on the rough roads. She kept her eyes straight ahead, not once in my direction. Before we got to the dirt road we needed, I glanced over at her hands. The drawstring on her purse was one big knot where she'd twisted it around to hold her nerves. My pulse picked up, knowing we were headed someplace we shouldn't.

The road was coarse and full of holes, and I didn't know which to worry about the most—whether the buggy would shake apart, or the mule would step in a hole and break his leg. Mama grabbed tight and held on. There wasn't much around, as I'd suspected, but up ahead I saw smoke and knew we were getting close to wherever.

Mama looked down at the map again. We soon hit a clearing and a line of small wooden houses with the brightest whitewash I'd ever seen. "Here," Mama said, pointing to one near the middle. Out in front sat a group of women, shucking corn under a big shade tree. They looked up, mumbling to each other when we stopped. One young lady sat with her skirt tied in a knot just below her knees. Her feet were bare and she wasn't wearing stockings. She stood and walked toward us. I recognized her honey-colored skin right away. It was Ruth, the Catholic girl that Ethan had been seeing in secret.

"You're Ethan's brother, aren't you? Is he all right?"

"That's what we came to ask you," Mama said, stepping down from the buggy.

"You're his ma?" Ruth asked.

Mama nodded, staring Ruth straight in the eyes.

"I haven't seen him," Ruth said, her voice soft and sad. "I've been worried."

Mama kept her face taut. "So have I. I heard you were hiding him out here."

Ruth smoothed a clump of sweaty hair away from her cheek. "Not here. No, he's not here, I swear it."

"I won't listen to that kind of talk. You can promise, but don't use that word. To swear is a sin."

Mama took her Baptist upbringing more serious than anyone I know. And she wasn't afraid to correct anybody who twisted her beliefs. Seems like the only person who'd ever got by with sinning was Ethan. Mama had a powerful lot of tolerance for his drinking. But that was all.

"I promise," Ruth said. "I haven't even gotten a letter. I miss him."

I could see that Ruth was telling the truth because a lie usually shows up in a person's eyes. Ruth's eyes were as dark as the night forest, but I could tell that no lie was residing in them.

Mama still stood, straight and proud. I could only guess what she must be thinking. Then she reached out and touched the small silver crucifix that hung on Ruth's necklace. "I miss him, too." She turned quickly and stepped back up into the buggy. "Let's go, Jesse."

Papa never even knew we'd gone. He was fired up about the town hall meeting that night, and spent his time slamming things around and talking to himself. After supper he took off. I sat with Mama for a while, then checked Ethan's room. More shirts were gone. Pud had been back to get his paycheck. Leather whined next to the window, so I went out on the porch to feed him. I saw Jackson coming out of the privy, heading back to the shack. I thought he'd have gone into town by now. I wondered if Papa had asked him to stay here to protect us, or if he just needed a night at home for a change. Or maybe he was just trying to avoid that meeting in town.

"Shhhh, Leather, stay real quiet." Like a bandit, I slipped into the darkness. I managed to get to the barn without making too much noise, even though the horses were restless in their stalls. I climbed up to my pallet in the loft. The hay felt soft and relaxing, but I was determined to stay awake.

I lay there a good hour watching the shack. Occasionally,

Jackson would stick his head out and look around. But mostly, he paced the room. His shadow passed back and forth like the pendulum on a clock. His restlessness had me squirming, too. *What are you up to, Jackson?*

I'm not sure exactly what time it was, but somewhere after ten o'clock, I heard horses. Two rough-looking men rode to Jackson's door. He came out and greeted them like they were expected. Once the light hit them I recognized their faces. Buster Caulden and Dale Finch, Ethan's poker buddies. Jackson snuck a glance back and forth, wary that someone might be watching. Why didn't he want to be seen? Leather ran out barking and growling, but Jackson petted his neck, trying to hush him up.

I lay still as a possum as the barn door creaked open. I didn't breathe.

Jackson swept in for his horse. But just as he reached the stall, he stopped. Did he sense me there? He looked around, checking the other stalls. Then his gaze slowly drew upward. Fear lit through me like a brush fire. *Does he know I'm up here?*

He took two steps toward the ladder, then retraced his steps back to the stall. Quietly, he led his horse out, and I let out all the air that had ballooned inside me.

I didn't move for a good five minutes after the three men rode off. My mind raced, wondering where they were headed. Maybe I was trying too hard to put faces to the fence-cutters. But this definitely smelled like trouble.

CHAPTER FOURTEEN

I **HAD PLANNED TO TELL PAPA** the next morning
about the company Jackson was keeping. 'Course there was no
guarantee he'd listen to me this time. But Papa was slamming
things and talking to himself more than the night before. So
Mama and I stayed out of his way. Good thing he didn't find
out about me taking Mama to Ruth's house. He'd tan me with
a strap, then hang me up by my toes. And besides, telling
him about Jackson probably wouldn't do no good. He'd likely
shrug it off and say the two men were just Jackson's buddies
from town. Papa never listened to me anyway, and trying to
explain things to him today would be like trying to reason
with a hornet. I'd just get stung.

I did most of my chores, then rode out to the back where
Jackson was working. He was making good progress on
mending that fence, and I hated to see it. On the one hand, I
believe a man has a right to fence his property. On the other

hand, finishing that fence would invite more trouble. Trouble with a capital T.

Jackson waved to me as he walked over. His hair and shirt were both dripping wet. It felt hot enough to cause that much sweat, but I figured more than likely he'd doused himself with water from the canteen to cool off.

The fence stretched long and taut. I ran my finger down the slick, twisted strands of wire, and stopped at one thorny barb. The whole thing wasn't much thicker than Mama's knitting yarn, yet it had the power and sting of a whip. Jackson must have read my thoughts. "A whole lot of fuss being made over this, huh?" he said.

"If everyone were just fussing, there wouldn't be so much trouble. Why are people so desperate?" I asked, anxious for his answer.

"Desperate times."

I should have known he'd figure a way to dance around my question.

Leather came trotting up with a rabbit skin in his mouth. He seemed mighty proud of that find. When I ignored him, he sat in the shade and played with the hide, pulling and tugging and gnawing.

"The ranchers held a meeting last night," I said to Jackson. "I think they're planning something." I waited for his reaction. His expression never even twitched. "What do you think should happen?" I prodded.

"I think it should rain."

I was getting nowhere. But there had to be some way to trap him.

We didn't speak for a few minutes. I helped him right a leaning fence post, and tugged a strand of wire for him. Then I asked the question that was itching me the whole time.

"Where do you head off to when you're gone so long at night?"

Jackson stopped and wiped the sweat from his forehead. "Did your papa send you out here to ask me that?"

"Nope, I just wanted to know myself."

"I work for your papa. I'll let him ask me the questions."

"But I thought Papa loaned you the rifle to protect the ranch. A lot of good that'll do if they come ripping up the fence again and you're not here! And you saw the note. Next time, they'll come after Papa."

Jackson shook his head. "Why don't you let me and your papa worry about that?"

"But it doesn't make any sense! You'd think a man out punching and driving cows all day would be too tired to ride out at night destroying people's property."

"Not all the cutters are free-range cowmen," Jackson said. "Many of them are cutthroats and bandits hired to do the work."

I thought about the wanted posters I'd seen at the post office. The sketches of savage outlaws with deep scars and fierce eyes that burned right through you. It gave me the shivers to think any of those scoundrels could be slinking around our property at night.

"And how much money do you think a cutthroat or bandit would make for pulling a job like that?"

Jackson pitched his hammer on the ground and stared at

me like a man ready to fight. "I'm sure I wouldn't know the answer to that, son! You got any more smart questions?"

I'd been caught in my own trap. Jackson knew I was testing him. If he was a fence-cutter I wouldn't weasel it out of him. But I didn't want to back down now.

"Why are you rebuilding this fence when you know trouble's brewing?"

"Because your papa asked me to."

"But he told you to take your time. He didn't tell you to finish it."

Jackson picked the hammer up off the ground. "Sure he did. This morning."

I didn't know what to say. I rode away from there like a streak of fire. Leather ran after me, rabbit pelt still in his mouth.

Inside the barn, I grabbed the currycomb and brushed my horse with hard fierce strokes. White foam sprayed from his flanks and settled on my pants. I didn't care. I wanted to scream.

Why can't Papa see what's going on under his own nose? Why does he trust Jackson so much? Why can't it just rain?

I shoved out of the barn and over to the shack. I hated the sight of it. I hated everything! I kicked the dirt. I kicked the rocks. And I kicked the shack so hard I hoped it would fall down. I kicked it harder and harder until the windows rattled and the front door swung open. When I couldn't muster up enough strength to kick anymore, I sat down by the door and buried my face in my arms.

Leather came up about then with the rabbit skin between his teeth. He wanted to play tug-o-war.

"Not now, Leather."

He rolled on his side, panting hard, then offered the rabbit pelt to me as a gift to cheer me up. I reached down and rubbed his sleek brown skin. "Come on, boy. Let's get you a bowl of water."

As I reached to close the door to the shack, something caught my eye. I swallowed hard as my heart hammered against my ribs. Then I bent down for a better look. Lying on the floor, up under the cot, was something that definitely didn't belong there! Jackson had a secret. And now I had proof.

CHAPTER FIFTEEN

I **SLOWLY PUSHED THE DOOR** open wider and crawled on hands and knees to get a better look. Jackson had stored a few things under his bunk. A couple of changes of clothes, his saddlebag, and a wooden box. But there was a tool placed under there, too—a tool that didn't belong to Papa.

Jackson was hiding a pair of wire cutters.

I pulled them out and snipped at the air a couple of times. Now I had him. I could convince Papa for sure that Jackson was up to no good. Or could I?

I was trying to decide whether to slip the wire cutters in my back pocket or put them back under the bunk when I heard someone approaching. I had to think fast! I barely had enough time to flatten myself into a straight line and roll under the cot. I knocked Jackson's things around as I pushed my way under, and bumped my head on the wooden box. The blanket hung down enough to hide me. Then I saw Mama's shoes and the bottom of her flower-print dress as she passed by the shack on her way to the hen house. She paused a moment, leaning in, then closed the door behind her. I waited until her footsteps faded and my heart stopped racing before coming out from under the cot.

Jackson had wire cutters and I had evidence, but a new thought occurred to me. How could I present them to Papa without looking like a sneak and a thief? I figured it was best for me to just slide them back under Jackson's bunk and get out before I got myself into a bigger mess of trouble. I could always formulate a plan once I was on safer ground. I leaned over and shoved the wire cutters back under the cot. They clunked against the wooden box. I started to get up and leave, but something gnawed at my insides. My attention was drawn back to the floor under the bunk. What in the world did Jackson keep in that box?

I thought about Mama saying, "Curiosity killed the cat," but this cat needed skinning. I reached under, my fingers touching the rough wood. As I pulled at the box, a crow flittered by the door, causing me to jerk back. I grabbed my heart and took a few breaths to settle my nerves. Then I yanked the box out and tugged at the lid. I should have known. Locked. I used my pocketknife to fiddle with the latch, but I worried that I might break the point off in it. I folded the knife, stuck it back in my pocket, then reached for Jackson's saddlebag. Sweat dripped from my fingers. I lifted the flap, quickly rummaged through it. For the first time, luck was on my side. I brought up a round iron key ring with three dangling keys. I clasped them in my fist to quiet the noise. The smallest key looked like it would fit the box. It did. The latch opened with a quiet click, and I carefully raised the lid.

I don't know what I'd expected to find in there, but it sure wasn't this. Lying cradled in the brown silk lining was a Colt 45 six-shooter! The fanciest gun I'd ever laid eyes on. The long slender barrel shone brighter than polished spurs, and the pearl handle was as white as a cloud.

Even in that Texas heat, a chill danced up my spine. Jackson had told Papa he didn't have a gun. He flat-out *lied*. And if he lied about that, what else had he lied about? Not much, I guessed, considering how he'd never answered any of my questions. Jackson was a man of secrets. And a man with secrets is a man to be feared.

I heard footsteps through the back window. I quickly closed the lid and placed the box back where I found it. Then, just as I tiptoed to the door, I heard Jackson's voice right outside it. "Hey, Old Leather Dog. What're you doing here?"

My heart banged so hard I was afraid he could hear it. If Jackson caught me in here, he just might use that six-shooter on me! I backed away from the door just as it started to open, creaking like a coffin lid. My coffin. I had no place to hide, and no excuse to be in here. Then I heard Jackson's voice again. "Good afternoon, Mrs. Wade. Can I give you a hand with those eggs?"

I didn't wait for Mama's answer. I quietly hurried to the back window, pushed aside the flour sack curtains, and dove through. I ran fast as a roadrunner straight into the privy, and pretended to be just coming out when I saw Jackson walking alongside Mama, carrying her egg basket for her. He narrowed his eyes, giving me a scowling look as they passed. I glared right back at him, calling his bluff. Now I knew his secret.

CHAPTER SIXTEEN

JACKSON WASN'T THE ONLY MAN with secrets. Papa had gone into town that morning, but what he did after that was a mystery. He didn't fuss or complain or rub his forehead in worry during supper that night. He seemed tired but cheerful. When we asked how his day was, he just said, "Productive."

I knew I couldn't bring up Jackson's lie or the six-shooter. Not because Papa wouldn't listen, but because Papa's cheerfulness put a calm across Mama's face that I hadn't seen in quite some time. No matter what, I didn't want Mama upset again. I'd just have to handle things on my own.

It seemed the barn was becoming my second home, and spying on Jackson was becoming a chore. I crawled into the hayloft and creaked the door open just a speck. There was no moon tonight to help me, but I had no trouble making out Buster and Dale when they rode up to the shack.

"You ready?" I heard Dale ask.

Jackson was sneaking those looks again. Guess he worried

that Papa had put two and two together and knew it equaled trouble. "As ready as I'll ever be," he answered.

He slipped into the barn, checking every corner. If he decided to look up in the loft, I was ready. I had the pitchfork laying next to me just in case.

But Jackson didn't bother. He got onto his horse, and they all headed for the horizon.

I quickly saddled my horse, then Leather and I followed.

I hung back as much as I could, mostly following their dust trail. Being in the hill country has its advantages, but I couldn't help wondering if the three men weren't on to me—sitting and waiting just over the next slope. My heart jumped to my throat and I could feel it pumping faster than a jackrabbit. My palms were sweaty and slipping on the reins. Could've been from the heat. Could've been from fear. Probably both.

I'd be dumber than a turkey to get caught now, but I had to keep going. Leather trotted along, sniffing at the dirt and jerking his head at the sound of every owl or bullfrog. Then, just as I rounded the curve by the dead oak, I pulled the reins hard and came to a fast stop. I could see men off in the distance, gathered in front of an old rickety house. I hid my horse behind some bushes and climbed the oak, flattening myself against one of the twisted limbs. I had to be careful, since there were no leaves to hide me.

I couldn't make out their faces, but I was pretty sure one of them was Jackson. His white shirt gleamed in the night. The other men were in dark clothes, harder to see. And it wasn't just the three of them anymore. They'd met up with two other guys who waved their arms and fidgeted about. I couldn't hear what they were saying, but occasionally some laughter would drift my way.

Then Leather spotted them. "No," I whispered. But it was too late. Why didn't I tether that dog before getting this far? He burst into a full run, barking and growling and kicking up dust. I couldn't whistle him back, so I slid partially down the limb, scratching my face and hands, and hid behind the larger part of it. It cracked and swayed as I gripped the jagged bark. My hands were on fire, but I didn't let go.

Leather stopped growling. I peeked around to see him wagging his tail as Jackson and a couple of the other men rubbed and patted his head. They strained their necks and looked in my direction. I laid my face on the tree, praying they wouldn't see me. I could barely breathe. I clamped my eyes shut, knowing they'd be riding up to find me. I waited, but I never heard the horses coming this way. I chanced another look. They were still just standing around.

After a few minutes all five men stepped into the old house, then I jumped down, got on my horse, and hauled out of there like a coyote with his tail on fire.

Once I was home, I crept into Ethan's room and sat down on the floor, hugging my knees. The pounding in my heart began to slow, and my face and hands stung from the scrapes and scratches of the dead oak. I needed to wash up, but I just couldn't move.

I leaned back against the wall and took everything in. The quilt, the curtains, the kerosene lamp—I was smothered in Ethan's presence and suffocating from loneliness. *If only Ethan would walk through that door,* I thought.

Then someone did.

CHAPTER SEVENTEEN

"**PUD! WHAT IN TARNATION** are you doing here this time of night?"

Pud grinned. "I come to get that blue flannel shirt for Mama to wrap the new baby in."

"Brother or sister?" I asked, my voice weak as water.

Pud's smile covered the room. "A new brother. Plug-ugly little critter to boot. But that makes five of us boys now, and we outnumber my sisters." He squinted and held his fists up like he was going to box clear air. "They'll think twice before bossing us around." He pulled the flannel shirt from the closet. I didn't protest. It was old and faded, and the shirttail was as ragged as Pud's overalls. He eyed those alligator boots again before shutting the door.

"Before you clean everything out," I said, "you should know that Ethan *will* be back."

Pud looked at me strange, studying my cuts and scrapes. "Lordy, Jesse, did you get in a rassling match with a bobcat?"

"Yep," I said, thinking that was all the explaining he needed.

"Looks like that bobcat won," he said, strutting out the door.

I was careful next morning for Mama not to see me. I didn't know how I'd explain the scratches on my face, which had scabbed over in the night and now looked like tiny purple stitches. I dressed quickly and slipped out of the house. I figured I'd get on with my chores and try to forget about the problems plaguing our house right now. But when I opened the barn door, I ran right smack dab into Jackson Slater. So much for avoiding the plague.

"What happened to your face?" he asked, narrowing his eyes.

"None of your business," I answered, walking away.

"That's just the problem, boy. I think you got hurt *because* of my business."

That was all I could take. I needed it out in the open. "So, what is your business, Jackson? I thought you were here to help us out, but you're just helping yourself out. If Papa knew what you really were, you'd be out on your hind end faster than a raccoon on a rotten apple. A rotten apple!"

Jackson put his hands on his hips and shook his head. He snorted a small laugh. "If your papa knew what I really was, huh? So tell me, Jesse. I'm listening. What am I?"

"A rotten apple!" I screamed.

I tried to hurry away, but Jackson grabbed my arm and

spun me around to face him. "You never answered my question, Jesse. How'd you hurt your face?"

I looked him straight in the eyes. "I cut my face on some tree bark last night."

"What were you doing in a tree?"

Although I could never lie to Mama, I didn't have any problem making up a whopper for the likes of him. I just wanted to satisfy his curiosity and get on with the day. "I heard a noise outside. Thought I'd go check it out in case the fence-cutters had come back. I figured that shiny new barbed wire was just calling out to them. The noise turned out to be a wild boar that got onto our property. He chased me up a tree, and I stayed there until he left."

"You were treed by a wild boar?" Jackson asked, looking doubtful.

"What else could I do? I didn't have a gun."

Jackson considered that for a moment. "What good's a gun if you can't pull the trigger?" he said with a smirk.

We just stood there staring at each other for a moment. I'm sure Jackson saw right through me.

"You better be more careful in the future," he said. "Your mama already lost one son. It'd just kill her to lose another."

His words echoed more of a threat than a precaution. I couldn't stomach another minute of him. I turned and kicked up some dust, walking away. I heard him calling out behind me.

"You hear me, Jesse? You best watch out!"

By some small miracle, I managed to stay clear of Jackson the rest of the day. I managed to stay clear of Mama, too. I didn't want her fussing over my bruises and cuts, mollycoddling me like a baby in short pants. And I avoided Papa, but not by a miracle. He'd gotten up early and headed into town again. He'd been riding in a lot lately, probably cooking up something with the other ranchers. They couldn't sit back and wait for the governor to do something. But I was scared because Papa had more problems than he knew about, and I had to figure a way to tell him.

Darkness crept up like a robber that night. I was pitching hay in the barn when suddenly it was too dark to see. Strange thing. No one had called me in for supper. My body ached as I headed for the house. I'd thrown myself into my chores to keep from thinking. And because Papa wasn't home, I'd had extra work to do.

I smelled supper burning on the stove. Mama was sitting in the living room, wringing a handkerchief in her hands and sobbing, a lot like the night Ethan left.

I knelt by her and stroked her hair, afraid she'd snap like a twig.

"What's wrong, Mama?" I asked in a whisper.

"He's gonna get himself killed."

I felt the panic rising again, but I waited a moment before asking. "Who?"

"Your papa!" she cried. "More fences were cut last night. Everyone's angry. He just left here with some men. He took the shotgun. You should have seen him, Jesse. He had the devil in him. I ran out to the shack to look for Jackson, but he wasn't there. I don't know what to do." She laid her forehead on the heel of her hand.

Of all the things God put in our heads, decisions are the worst. I felt as torn as wheat in a thrasher. But I had to decide something—fast!

"I'm sure it'll be okay, Mama. You're just upset about nothing." But I knew better. I knew what kind of danger lay ahead. I wanted to get out of there quick and warn Papa. He was no match for Jackson and his gang of fence-cutting fiends.

"Don't worry. Things will be all right." I turned to leave.

"Jesse! Where are you going?" Mama asked, flustered and frightened.

"It's okay, I'm just going to move the pot off the stove."

And since I couldn't lie to Mama, I did lift the pot off the stove … on my way out the door.

CHAPTER EIGHTTEEN

I RAN OUTSIDE, INTO THE NIGHT, with one thought screaming in my head. I had to find Papa before he found the fence-cutters. I had to warn him about Jackson and his dirty lies. I had to stop this madness tonight.

I raced to the barn to saddle my horse, Leather trailing at my heels. I grabbed for the harness when another thought hollered out to me. Should I leave here without a gun?

A wad of spit hung in my throat. Better to be safe than sorry.

Jackson had the rifle. Papa had the shotgun. But there was still one weapon left … I hoped. I ran to the shack and kicked the door open. I fumbled in the dark for the wooden box Jackson had stashed under his bunk. I slid it out and into the light that sifted in through the doorway. Luckily, the lid was still unlocked. As I raised it, the six-shooter gleamed through the shadows. I lugged it out of the box with a trembling hand.

My mouth was dry as dust. But this was no time to turn yellow. I had to help Papa.

I tucked the gun into the waist of my trousers, then searched for extra bullets. I figured Jackson would have kept them in the box, too. It was still too dark to see, so I placed my hand inside it and felt along the lining on the bottom. Nothing there—smooth as Old Leather Dog's belly. As I zipped my fingers across the top lining, something pricked my finger like a cactus needle. I quickly pulled my hand out, shaking it hard. I slid the box even closer to the doorway, hoping it would be lighter. The silk lining bulged inside the lid, and when I ripped it apart, something like a silver dollar popped out and clinked on the floor. I picked it up and held it close to my face.

It was a rough round badge with a star, made from Mexican pesos. Carved onto it were the words *TEXAS RANGERS*.

I leaned back against the wall and rubbed my forehead to make better sense of things. Jackson had lied all right, but not about being a fence-cutter. This badge said it all.

More than ever, I needed to find Papa. Jackson might be able to wrangle the fence-cutters, but not if Papa interfered. What if he and his posse were to find Jackson? Most likely they'd shoot first and ask questions later, and by then it'd be too late. And how would Papa feel if he found out he'd fired his bullets straight into a Texas Ranger?

I didn't have time to find extra bullets. I just hoped the Colt 45 was fully loaded. As I was about to ride away, Leather looked up. "Not this time," I said to him, worried that he'd give me away. Plus, I didn't want to put him in any danger.

One dog was already dead because of me. I wouldn't lose this one. I found a stick lying on the ground and pitched it into the barn. When Leather ran for it, I shut the barn door, locking him in.

"What's going on, Jesse?"

I jumped like a grasshopper, turning around to face the voice. "Good gracious, Pud! It's dark. What in tarnation are you doing here?"

"Earning some money," he said. "Real money."

I leaned against the barn door, Leather scratching on the other side. "Earning money?"

"Yep," Pud said, looking proud. "Jackson gave me a nickel to watch you. Said if I kept you occupied, and here at home, he'd give me another nickel when he got back."

"Pud," I said, more anxious than a treed coon, "you ain't getting that other nickel. I've got to go."

Pud's smile turned over and he held up his fists. "You ain't going anywhere, Jesse."

"Don't do this." I tried to sound angry, but I couldn't chance Mama hearing and coming out here.

"Jesse, I'll knock you silly. Now Jackson gave me a duty, and I aims to see it through."

I didn't want to hurt Pud. I just needed to outsmart him. Leather was scratching harder on the door, whining to get out. Then it occurred to me. "You know those alligator boots of Ethan's?"

Pud lowered his fists, nodding.

"They're worth more than a nickel."

"You givin' me Ethan's boots?" Pud asked.

"If you let me go right now."

Pud's smile returned and he stepped out of the way.

I raced like a demon toward the old house where Jackson had met up with the fence-cutters. Things were starting to make sense.

I rounded the curve by the dead oak and saw three horses tied out front. The yellow glow of a lantern colored one window. I wanted to warn Jackson about Papa, but I wasn't dumb enough to walk into a death trap. I tied my horse to the oak and snuck the rest of the way to the house.

I crawled on my belly past the ramshackle porch and up to the window. I could hear voices inside but couldn't make out the words. As slowly as I could, I rose up to the corner of the window and peeked inside.

The room was dusty and dim, and except for a couple of chairs and a rickety table, it was practically empty. I could see Jackson pacing the floor, talking to Dale. Dale was slinging a bottle around and grinning through wet lips. I pressed my ear to the window, trying to hear. Words fluttered here and there like torn paper. "Fences … guns … varmints … tonight." Whatever they were planning, it was big.

The weight of the six-shooter tugged at my trousers. I untucked my shirt and shifted the gun a little. I looked in again to see Dale take a swig of whatever rotgut was in that bottle. He held it out to Jackson, but Jackson waved it away. He went back to pacing.

It was obvious they were waiting. But for what? I had to

figure a way to get in there without anyone seeing me but Jackson. He had to know what dangers were waiting.

Something else was obvious. There were three horses tied up in front, but there were only two men inside the house.

That's when I heard a twig snap behind me.

"Don't move," a gruff voice threatened.

I stood still as a tree stump. Then he jabbed the cool barrel of a revolver against my temple.

CHAPTER NINETEEN

"**LOOKEE, LOOKEE HERE!**" Buster said, squeezing my arm and shoving me through the doorway. "We got company."

Jackson's face wilted when he saw me stumbling in. "Jesse, what are you doing here?"

I didn't answer. I guess having a gun pointed at my head made me tongue-tied.

"So what d'you think?" Buster said with a slobbery grin. "Should we give the boy some wire cutters and put him to work?" He laughed like the fool he was.

"Shut your mouth!" Jackson said. "This presents some new problems." He looked at me again with questioning eyes.

"Well, you better come up with a solution to *this* problem right now," Dale blurted, "because we're gonna ride shortly." He slammed his bottle down on the wobbly table and placed his hands on his hips.

I turned my head slowly and looked at the gun Buster was

aiming at me. I wasn't about to speak until it was back in its holster. Jackson got the message.

"Buster, put that thing away," he ordered.

"I might as well," Buster said, grinning like a possum. "It ain't even loaded."

Then he butted against me hard, knocking me to the floor. I managed to catch myself with my hands, thankful nobody could see the six-shooter hidden under my shirt.

Jackson kicked an old wooden chair toward me. "Have a seat." He leaned forward, resting his hands on his thighs, and glared straight into my eyes. "One more time. What are you doing here, Jesse?"

"I came looking for you," I whispered. "There's something you need to know."

"And there's something you need to know," he whispered back. "Boys that come looking for trouble usually find it. And they could get themselves killed."

He still looked me in the eye while he spoke to Dale and Buster. "Either of you boys have some rope?"

"Indeed," Buster said, rubbing his hands together. "Never know when I'll get the urge to hogtie something."

Buster went out to his horse, then came back with a length of rope. "I'm going to enjoy this," he said.

"No you're not." Jackson took the rope from his hands, and I was mighty thankful. He pulled my arms through the slats in the chair back and wound the rope around my wrists. I waited for the burn as he knotted it, but he tied it so loose I could barely feel it at all. It was the kind of knot you'd tie around something you weren't planning to keep.

"This'll hold him till we get back."

The door creaked and all three men turned quickly, Jackson reaching for the rifle. I expected to see Papa and the other ranchers stepping in with guns drawn, ready to haul these varmints away. What I didn't expect to see was Leather trotting in, especially since he's trained to stay outside. I could only guess that Mama had gone to the barn looking for me and let him out. Leather slunk toward me, knowing something was wrong.

"Oooo-whee!" Dale said, letting out a sigh of relief. "Why it's just Ole Slick, his mangy dog."

Leather stretched out by my feet and laid his head on his paws. Shortly, there was another noise out front. This time it was horses.

"They're here!" Buster yelled. "Let's go."

The three men headed for the door. Jackson glanced back at me. His face looked like that of a man torn up inside, not knowing for sure if he was doing the right thing.

"I've got to tell you something," I said.

Jackson just turned and walked out the door.

I sat quiet for a moment, listening to them mount their horses and ride away. They must have been joining up with the two men I saw them with the other night.

But there was no time to ponder. I had to get away quick. I rubbed my wrists together, trying to slip the rope off. Jackson had tied it loosely, but not loose enough. I couldn't pull my hands through. The rope stung as I wiggled and tugged. No use. I looked around for something to cut it with and saw Dale's whiskey bottle propped up on the table, about half full.

"Move, Leather," I said, trying to stand up with the chair resting on my back. It wasn't easy to stay balanced, but I slowly crept over to the table. I plopped the chair down and looked straight at that bottle. This was going to take some doing. I straightened my knees again. In a cramped standing position, I turned around. I don't know what made me think I could reach that bottle. I only banged the chair legs against the tabletop. I turned back toward the bottle again. Maybe I could grab it with my teeth? Nope. I came up short by just a few inches. I plopped back on the chair, looking and wondering.

I always thought of myself as a pretty smart fellow, but even the smartest folks don't have brilliant ideas right away. Mine finally came. I stretched my feet out, placed them up against that shaky old table, and rocked it back and forth on its four legs. I was careful not to kick it. I didn't want the bottle to roll off and shatter. It swayed back and forth like a cradle, and the bottle tilted and rolled forward. I dropped my feet and caught it in my lap. The smell burned my nostrils as some of the whiskey spilled onto my pants. I was a lot closer to that bottle now, but still couldn't reach it.

With a few deep breaths to steady myself, I slowly opened my knees, letting the bottle slip through them and onto the floor. Luckily, it landed straight as a soldier.

I whipped the chair around and slumped down as far as I could. The bottle was just within my grasp. I held it tightly with my right hand and banged it as hard as I could on the chair leg. It took seven or eight tries before the bottle broke. Leather flinched, and the smell of cheap whiskey singed the air. My fingers still clasped what was left of the bottle—a neck with a few jagged shards sticking out. I turned it up and sawed the rope. I worked at a furious pace. Sweat rolled into my eyes and I tried to blink it away. I continued to cut at the rope, but couldn't seem to make progress. My hands burned like a branding iron. I craned my neck and looked over my shoulder. I'd sliced up more of my flesh than I had the rope. I dropped the bottleneck to the ground.

I sat for a moment, panting harder than Old Leather Dog. "Awwwww!" I screamed, grabbing the rope that trailed from my wrists and whipping it up and down behind me. Leather jumped up like he'd spotted a rabbit. He dove for the rope and yanked it with his teeth. It was time to play tug-o-war.

Between his yanking and the blood gooping up my wrists, the rope managed to slip off. I was free! But wild screams echoed from the front yard, turning my blood to frost. *What was that?* I gripped the rope tight in my bloody hands. Then I waited for the worst.

CHAPTER TWENTY

"**B**RING HIM IN!" DALE SHOUTED, kicking the door open. I saw Billy, the other poker player from the saloon, holding Jackson's rifle as he slipped in behind Dale. Then Jackson and Buster entered, both carrying a man gushing a river of blood. His pants were torn and his leg was mangled like a butchered cow. I fought hard to swallow the vomit that shot into my throat. I could see clean through to his bone. The man clutched his leg and wailed in agony as they set him down on the table. Leather jumped up, propping his front paws next to the man, then licked his face. He pushed Leather back and turned his head my way.

My heart stopped. "Ethan!"

Tears streaked down his face. His pleading look told me he wasn't as surprised to see me as I was to see him. But he was half crazy from the pain. "Bear traps!" he yelled. "The old coot set out bear traps!"

Billy handed Jackson his rifle, and Jackson leaned it on the chair near mine. "We'll pour whiskey on the wound. That'll help till we can get him to the doctor," he said, looking around. Then he saw the broken bottle and the blood behind my chair.

"No doctors!" Dale shouted.

"What?" Jackson roared.

"That'd be the same as turning ourselves in," Dale said. "And I ain't planning on going to prison."

"He'll die if we don't get him to a doctor," Jackson protested. He took off his hat and slicked his dark hair back with his hand. He looked to be searching for ideas. "We can send Jesse off to bring the doctor back here."

"Are you crazy?" Buster shouted. "We're not going down like this." He walked next to Dale, and the two men stood shoulder to shoulder to show they'd put up a fight.

Ethan writhed on the table, his chest rising and falling in heavy spasms. He was still looking at me as his eyes glassed over. "Help me, Jesse."

I dropped the rope from my hands and stood up. I had to do something fast. I felt the Colt 45 resting against my side.

Billy cowered in a corner of the room, chewing his nails. He looked to be about Ethan's age, but I wasn't sure whose side he was on. He wasn't arguing to get Ethan to a doctor, but he wasn't complaining against it either.

I listened to the arguing for a few more seconds when I finally found my voice. "You can all just kiss my foot! I'm going for the doctor!" I walked toward the door with my head high, but Buster ran up and before I knew what was happening, he'd kicked my feet out from under me. I went sprawling to the ground face first. My shirttail flew up and the six-shooter fell out of my pants and skidded across the floor.

Leather barked and growled as Buster picked up the gun. He kicked Leather in the side, sending him whining in the corner near Billy.

"Where'd a little pipsqueak like you get such a fancy gun?" Buster asked.

For a brief moment, Jackson registered surprise, then he slowly reached his hand out toward Buster. "Hand it over before somebody gets hurt."

"Somebody's already hurt!" I cried, pointing to Ethan who was now lying perfectly still. "We've got to do something!"

"The only thing you're going to do is sit down and shut your trap!" Buster said, ushering me back to the chair.

Dale walked up to Buster and slid two fingers down the barrel of the Colt 45. "That's one fine weapon," he said. "And six rounds, too. Got to admire that. Yep, I think we've got enough bullets here for the two of us to finish this business and make a clean getaway."

Billy bolted for the door, but Buster cocked the gun and aimed it before he could get halfway.

"You ain't going nowhere," Buster said.

Billy froze in his steps. Then Buster slowly turned the gun on Jackson. "Okay, Mr. Fancy Talker, think you can talk your way out of this?"

Jackson didn't say a word. Instead, he slowly raised his hands in the air.

I'd learned a lot of things in the last few weeks, but the most valuable lesson was the one I'd just learned from Buster himself. I leaned back in my chair and kicked his feet right out from under him. He still held the six-shooter as he dropped to the ground, but in one swift move, I grabbed Jackson's rifle and aimed it with my bloody hands. Now Dale was the one backing away, holding his hands over his head. Buster tightened his grip on the Colt 45, but I stomped my boot down on his hand and held it there under my foot.

Dale stood stiff for a moment, and then the panicked look on his face began to melt and a big ugly grin took its place. "I've heard a lot about you, boy," he said, slowly lowering his hands. "Yes, sir. Ethan talked about you a lot."

I stared down the barrel of the rifle, right at Dale's chest.

"Yep, Ethan liked to talk about his *baby* brother. So proud … except for one thing. You really are a baby. He told us you ain't even got the guts to shoot a gun."

Dale slid his foot forward, but I tightened on the rifle and stepped down harder on Buster's hand. "Take Ethan out to the horses," I said to Jackson. My throat was dryer than this Texas summer, and my heart raced like a jackrabbit. They knew I was bluffing, that I couldn't shoot. But I kept a stern look, even though my trigger finger felt like butter.

Jackson reached for Ethan. I felt better hearing him moan as Jackson scooted him forward. Thank God he was still alive.

"You ain't going nowhere!" Dale yelled, pulling a knife from his belt and pointing it at Jackson. "Because I know sissy boy ain't gonna fire that gun."

"Shoot him, Jesse," Jackson said quickly.

It seemed like a sound solution, but my brain was still jumbled, and I couldn't let go of that image of Smokey, lying bloody and lifeless before me.

"Come on, boy," Dale said, still grinning. "Hand over the rifle."

My finger tightened on the trigger, and I heard Ethan moan again.

Dale slid another foot forward, and I brought my aim up … right between his eyes. This standoff had to end one way or another, but I wasn't liking my odds. My head burned like a fever and my hands trembled. The rifle felt as heavy as a bucket of rocks. Looking down the rod of that gun, Dale seemed smaller, like I was looking at him through a knothole. He grinned at me with his big crooked teeth and took another jab at Jackson.

The vision of Smokey faded, and it was Ethan I saw lying there, cold and dead. I thought about Mama. What would happen if Ethan really did die? There'd be no hope left for her at all. I clenched my jaw and took a deep breath. No one's putting my brother in a coffin. I moved my aim a bit to the left.

"Come on, Jesse, shoot him! Shoot!" Jackson urged.

A loud blast filled the room as the bullet whizzed by Dale's face, leaving a bloody stump where his ear used to be. He dropped the knife and grabbed the mangled sludge on the side of his head, hissing like a steam kettle.

I froze, too. It's amazing what a person can do when they have to. Reaching down, I pried the Colt 45 from Buster's crooked red fingers. He sneered.

"Here, Jackson!" I tossed it to him.

Jackson nodded toward the rope lying behind the chair. "So, tell me, Jesse," he said with a slight grin, "you got the urge to hogtie something?"

CHAPTER TWENTY-ONE

ETHAN STILL BREATHED—by a sheer miracle. We bandaged his leg with Billy's shirt and loaded him onto my horse.

"Ride fast," Jackson said, slapping the horse's rump. I rode out of there without a thought in my mind but getting Ethan to the doctor fast. The horse's hooves clapped against the silence of the still night. I could barely swallow, my throat dry and begging for water—like the cotton and the trees and the animals in this godforsaken Texas hell. My bloody hands stung as I held the reins. But I put my own misery aside. Time was ticking away. And so was Ethan's life.

The next two weeks were quiet ones. Mama and Papa didn't talk much. But the creases in Mama's face softened just from having Ethan home. Where else would he've gone? He needed looking after, and Mama kept busy doing just that. She wasn't doing the job alone though. Both Ruth and Mary Ann came to help. Normally he would have loved all the attention, but under the circumstances, he seemed defeated. He let the women fuss about anyway, telling him what to do, and helping him learn to walk on a crutch. Not an easy task for a man with just one leg.

But he wasn't the only one drawing attention. Just a few days after Ethan's homecoming, Papa asked me to take a ride with him. "Come on, son. This old farm can do without us for a while." I welcomed the chance to get away, even though there was no escaping my thoughts.

We rode into town, Papa sitting higher on the saddle than usual. It was hotter out than a griddle, but that didn't keep the twinkle out of his eyes. I couldn't figure what in tarnation had him so calm and content.

We hitched up in front of the barbershop, and I'd no sooner stepped off my horse when Papa came over and put his arm around my shoulder. He kept his eyes straight ahead, cocked his hat back some, and we entered just like that—side by side.

The usual crowd sat, reading the paper, playing checkers, and there was one man who appeared to be an actual paying customer. Mr. Tucker looked up and shot us a blinding grin. "Well, look who's here!" He plumb ignored that customer he'd all soaped up for shaving and came over to us, extending his hand.

Papa took his arm off my shoulder, and I figured it was to shake Mr. Tucker's hand. But he just took a step back instead. It was *my* hand Mr. Tucker wanted to shake. And he wasn't the only one. If I hadn't known my name before I went in there, I surely would have known it coming out. Everyone came to life suddenly, rushing over and saying, "Jesse, good to see you."

"Jesse, we heard you cornered them scoundrels!" "Jesse, you're one brave man, saving your brother and all." I especially liked hearing that. Knowing I'd saved Ethan was the only thing that kept me sane anymore.

Mr. Tucker eyed my hair, hanging down past my collar. "When you're ready for that haircut, Jesse, it's on the house."

"Not today," Papa said. "Jesse and I just came into town to pick up some rock salt. Thought we'd sit out on the porch tonight and crank up some ice cream."

I shoot a man and we celebrate? Especially a man like Dale—as slimy as the gunk in Mr. Tucker's spittoon. I only took off his ear. Ethan had lost half a leg.

Makes you think about the lengths a man will go to. I saved Jackson's and Ethan's life, and my own to boot. Action and reaction. I live it over and over in my head. It's all about survival. For the first time since Smokey died, I *had* to pull the trigger. And I'd done it. I guess we've all got fences to cut.

Mr. Tucker shook my hand again before we left. "He's a real chip off the old block, ain't he, Tom?"

"No, sir," Papa said, patting my back. "That kind of courage don't come from kin. Jesse's his own man."

I couldn't help but tack on a grin at that.

Papa and I got along better than ever, but he was like a cold stone when it came to Ethan. It seemed so backwards having two people living in the same house, yet carrying on like the other didn't exist. I was having to divide my time between them, not wanting either one to think I was taking sides.

Ethan's leg was slow to heal, but changing the dressing regularly and soaking it in Epsom salts seemed to do the trick. Before long he had a little more spirit about him. Before long, so did I.

As I helped him to the kitchen table, he looked up at me with a goofy smile. "I've got an idea."

"You're not going to suggest we go fishing, are you?"

He laughed. "Nope, but I was thinking we could throw some grub in a basket and have one of those picnics like we used to down by the crosswire."

That sounded like a good enough plan to me.

I helped him onto the quilt I'd spread out under the oak. Leather lay down, resting his head on the knee of Ethan's good leg. I got busy pulling the food out for us.

"Papa actually spoke to me this morning," Ethan said.

I wasn't sure if he was bragging or complaining. "What'd he say?"

"Pass me my pipe."

We both laughed out loud, and it was music to my ears.

"Papa will come around," I said.

Ethan shook his head. "I doubt it."

I wanted to say more, to encourage him, but he was probably right. Papa was one hard-headed old man. Hard-headed—just like Ethan. "You're lucky though. You got two girlfriends now, and that don't seem to bother Mama at all."

Ethan looked down at the nub of his leg. His pants were pinned up where it ended, just below the knee. "They're enjoying it now, but wait until some time passes. When they realize I can't take a walk with them ... dance with them ..." He turned his head and looked down.

I felt the heat rising to my cheeks and turned away, casting all my attention to Old Leather Dog.

"Jesse."

"Um-huh," I said, afraid to look up.

"I'm not staying."

That didn't surprise me. Not one bit. "Where will you go?"

"I don't know," he said. "But when my leg's totally healed, I can get a wooden one. Learn to walk properly. Then I'll figure it out from there. But I have to leave."

"You can always get a peg leg and become a pirate," I said, teasing.

"Naw, I'd just get seasick."

We ate there by the crosswire, looking out at the summer afternoon. Then Ethan pulled himself up higher where he sat. "You know, Jesse ... I never really thanked you."

"I didn't do nothing you wouldn't've done."

Ethan snickered, and I could tell his laugh was mingled with some tears. "You saved my life. Heck, I couldn't even do that. And I know how hard it was for you to fire that gun."

I shrugged, wondering if my face was as red as it felt. "I just did what I had to."

"No you didn't. You didn't have to do any of that. I probably wouldn't have."

I couldn't take it anymore. Hearing this sappy talk from my brother was too much for me to handle.

"Shut up and eat," I said, not looking up.

He reached over and clutched my arm. "Jesse. It doesn't matter that Papa don't speak to me. But I hear him talking to you. And about you. You sure did make him proud."

"I know," I said, finally glancing at his face.

He was looking at me with big eyes and a crooked grin. "You're the real son now. You ain't a shadow anymore."

He was right. I should have felt guilty, but I didn't. Being somebody felt good. "Try to act like a man," Mama had said. I'd tried. I'd tried my darnedest. And I'll be damned if I didn't pull it off.

It's funny how folks can come and go, in and out of people's lives. Sometimes it matters, like with Ethan. Sometimes it don't. Jackson disappeared and no one said much about it. He was gone quicker than a wink. Pud showed up to take his place with the chores, and I didn't feel one bit of regret passing off those alligator boots to him. Ethan didn't need them both anyhow. But Pud was good company to have around, even if he was always complaining about his sisters, or the baby crying, or how the latest rainmaker in town was a phony. I thought maybe he and Mary Ann should get together and have a tongue wagging contest. But I wouldn't know which one to place my bet on.

I felt bad that I never got to apologize to Jackson. Or to thank him for being on our side. But when a mysterious letter arrived in the mail for me, I knew exactly who'd written it before I tore open the envelope.

Dear Jesse,

Being a lawman is a tough job. You don't always know who to trust. Many times a lawman has to go against the law just to see that justice is served. Sometimes people are deceived, sometimes people get hurt.

I'm writing this to thank you. Not just for your help, but also for your silence. My job is a lot easier when folks don't know I carry this badge.

Because of you, Buster, Dale, and Billy are in jail. They'll be there for a long time. Luckily, I came in contact with many other fence-cutters there too. They're behind bars as well.

I saw no need to press charges against Ethan. He was never a real fence-cutter, just a mixed-up boy holding a grudge against his papa and trying to work off his gambling debts. Losing his leg was punishment enough.

Remember, you did humanity a favor. Dale's list of crimes stretched longer than the fences he cut. Trust me, Jesse, you not only saved our lives, but probably the lives of some future victims as well. The town citizens won't miss Dale Finch. Buster either, for that matter.

There aren't enough words invented to express how proud I am for the job you did helping me capture those outlaws. I've met many brave men in my time, but none braver than you. So why don't we make a deal? In a few years you ride out here to Waco and look me up. I think you'd make a darn fine Texas Ranger.

Sincerely,

Jackson Slater

Frontier Battalion, Company F

I read that letter twice, then sat, staring out the window. Nothing out there had changed, but something seemed different. Me. I didn't think I'd ever see things the same again. Leather nudged my arm, wanting to play tug-o-war, but I waved him away. That letter had given me so much to think about.

And then, just when I thought things couldn't get any better, they did. It rained.

AFTERWORD

The Texas Rangers and the Fence Cutters

Before 1875 in Texas, cattle roamed over thousands of acres of public land, and free grazing became a tradition. After 1875, however, an increasing farm populace tended to protect crops and other property with barbed wire fences which were resented by stock raisers. Cattle losses in droughts of the 1880s provoked such widespread cutting of fences that the Texas government recognized this as a crime and in 1884 enacted laws and measures to curb the practice. Texas Rangers were dispatched by the Governor at the call of County Judges and Sheriffs to apprehend the fence cutters. They operated from the Red River to the Rio Grande, and from the Panhandle to the Pine Woods of East Texas. Disguise and concealment were required, and one of the Rangers who won praise for his work pronounced it the most disagreeable duty in the world. The vigorous effort went on for some years. Finally, however, stockmen who had wanted to restore the open range were won over to fencing their own lands and using windmills to water their cattle herds. The Texas Rangers had in one more instance helped to stabilize life in the West.

I've always loved Texas history. Particularly history that relates to my family. During my early teens, I heard a story about my grandfather. He was born in 1860, and moved to Texas during the time of the Fence-Cutting Wars.

One evening, while sitting at home, several men rode up on horses. They called him out, asking, "Are you with us or agin' us?"

My grandfather replied, "I'm with you."

"Then get your horse and join us," one said.

My grandfather waved them off. "It's late, and I'm tired."

Again he was asked, "Are you with us or agin' us?"

"I'm with you," he assured them.

"Then come with us."

My grandfather mounted his horse and joined the men as they rode out to cut fences.

I was intrigued with the fence-cutters after that. Sadly, the only mention of them in my seventh-grade Texas history textbook was one simple paragraph. There hasn't been much written about the fence-cutters, and that's what inspired me to write Jesse's story.

FENCING

The war between the free-range cattlemen and landowning farmers and ranchers began with the invention of barbed wire.

To protect their crops, chickens, and other livestock, farmers tried a variety of fencing materials to border their properties. Early settlers relied on stone walls. But stone took up too much space, the walls were slow to complete, and the effort of building them was taxing on the workers.

They later relied on wood fences since they were easier to assemble. But wood could not stand up to frequent prairie fires. The fires not only consumed the fences, but destroyed replacement supplies as well. Wood was also prone to damage from insects and moisture rot. And it proved to be expensive as well.

A cheaper, more natural way to protect property was the use of hedge fencing. Thorny plants such as cactus and rose bushes were planted close together to form dense, prickly hedges. The practice of hedge fencing became so popular that the selling of plants and seeds became a viable business.

It was these natural, thorny fences that inspired the invention of barbed wire.

While a few men came up with their own ideas for "armored fencing," it was a farmer named Joseph Glidden who created and patented the type of barbed wire we are familiar with today. Glidden's barbed wire not only provided protection for cattle and crops, but was the least expensive form of fencing as well. Because the cost was so cheap, and the wire so easy to string, by the late 1870s barbed-wire fences stretched across acres and acres of Texas land.

THE FENCE-CUTTERS

Barbed-wire fences were a threat to cowmen who owned large herds of cattle but no property. These cattlemen felt it their God-given right to drive their herds to any creek, pond, or river for watering, and that the land should be open for grazing. But as barbed wire became increasingly popular, many landowners not only fenced their property, but also placed fences around the resources they needed for their livestock. Many times they fenced public property as well, blocking public roads, cutting off schools and churches, and interfering with mail delivery.

Unfortunately for the free-range cowmen, nature intruded, too. A drought in 1883 began a series of problems for both the landowners and the free-range cattlemen.

With prairie grasses diminishing, and river and creek beds drying up, the cattlemen required a wider range of land for their herds. Barbed wire made it nearly impossible to move them from one place to another.

Out of desperation, these free-range cattlemen clipped the fences to allow their cattle to pass. This act infuriated landowners, who simply rebuilt the fences. Thus began the Fence-Cutting Wars.

The fence wars grew, with reports of cut fences from Houston to El Paso. And while the clipping was originally done by the free-range cowmen, they soon turned to rougher hired hands to do the cutting for them. Armed gangs with names like Owls, Javelinas, or Blue Devils often cut fences at night. They sometimes left warnings and threats against rebuilding. And, at times, fenced pastures were burned.

By late 1883 damage to fences in Texas was calculated to be $20 million. News of the fence-cutters reached as far as Chicago. One Chicago newspaper held this headline:

HELL BREAKS LOOSE IN TEXAS!
Wire Cutters Destroy 500 Miles of Fence In Coleman County

On October 15, 1883, Governor John Ireland called for a special legislative session to meet on January 8, 1884, to amend the fencing laws. Several weeks later, lawmakers set penalties of one to five years in prison for cutting a fence, and two to five years for maliciously burning a pasture. They also authorized a misdemeanor law for fencing public lands or enclosing another's property without consent. Unlawful fences were required to be taken down within six months, and a gate was required for every three miles of fence that crossed public roads.

CHARACTERS

Crosswire is strictly a work of fiction, as are the characters I've created. But I was careful to write them true to the times.

Boys like Jesse were expected to do their share of farming chores, which generally included milking, gathering eggs, pitching hay, mending fences, picking cotton, and gathering crops. And Jesse's fear of shooting a gun would have been a great problem for a boy living in rural Texas in the 1880s. Guns were essential for hunting, a common way of supplying food. Young boys were taught to hunt deer, quail, squirrel, and boar. Guns were also needed for protection from dangerous prairie creatures like snakes, wild boar, and predatory coyotes that posed a threat to sheep and chickens.

Papa is a good example of a farmer protecting his property. In the 1880s small farms were generally about 120 to 160 acres. Farmers devoted much of that land to livestock such as cows, sheep, goats, and hogs. Raising cattle was a prosperous business at the time, cows selling for about five cents a pound.

A smaller portion of the farm was used for raising cotton (a common crop in Texas) and an assortment of vegetables. Planting and gathering crops required a great deal of time and effort. Because extra help was needed, farmers used sharecroppers to help with the task. In the novel, Pud and his family worked as sharecroppers on Jesse's farm before the crops dried up. A sharecropper was a worker who raised crops on a farm plot owned by the farmer. The small plot was payment for working the fields.

Jackson was inspired by a Texas Ranger named Ira Aten. Aten was charged with locating and capturing fence-cutters. Like Jackson, he often worked undercover as a ranch hand to do his job. Aten was not only successful in identifying fence-cutters, but he also helped to decrease the damage that was done.

Texas suffered another long drought in 1888, causing the practice of fence-cutting to surface again. Aten decided to take matters into his own hands and end it once and for all. He placed dynamite bombs along some of the fences in Navarro County. The dynamite had small wires attached as triggers, so that by cutting the barbed wire, it would ignite the dynamite. Aten was ordered to remove the bombs, but instead he set them off. Word spread, and out of fear, the act of cutting fences was reduced, and soon died out.

TEXAS RANGERS

The story of the Texas Rangers began in 1823. Stephen F. Austin, one of the founders of Texas, wrote that he would "...employ ten men ... to act as rangers for the common defense." This small group of men "ranged" around Austin's colony to protect settlers from Indian attacks. Since no threat was imminent, these rangers journeyed home to their families.

In 1835 when Texas was fighting for its independence, a council of government representatives created a "Corps of Rangers" to safeguard the land from enemies. These rangers furnished their own guns, horses, and equipment, and were paid $1.25 a day.

The Rangers were like police officers, making arrests anywhere within the state. And since there were so few of them, they didn't waste time with petty crooks and thieves, but instead tracked notorious Texas outlaws.

The requirements for being a Ranger were specific. He had to be young, in good physical shape, and brought up on a ranch or farm, giving him ample riding experience.

Rangers generally wore nice hats and durable boots, and used western-style saddles for their horses. Their early badges were forged from Mexican pesos.

On August 10, 1935, the Texas legislature created the Texas Department of Public Safety. The Texas Rangers are a part of this agency.

The Texas Rangers are the oldest law enforcement organization on the North American continent with statewide jurisdiction. They are still an important part of Texas law enforcement.

BIBLIOGRAPHY

Campbell, Randolph B. *Gone to Texas: A History of the Lone Star State.*
New York: Oxford University Press, 2003.

Krell, Alan. *The Devil's Rope: A Cultural History of Barbed Wire.*
London: Reaktion Books Ltd., 2002.

McCallum, Henry D., and Frances T. McCallum. *The Wire That Fenced the West.* Norman, OK: University of Oklahoma Press, 1965.

Preece, Harold. *Lone Star Man—Ira Aten: Last of the Old Texas Rangers.*
New York: Hastings House Publishers, 1960.

Wallace, Ernest, David M Vigness, George B. Ward, eds. *Documents of Texas History.* Austin, TX: Texas Historical Association, 2002.

Webb, Walter Prescott. *The Story of the Texas Rangers.*
Austin, TX: Encino Press, 1971.